The
Missing Pages

The Missing Pages

A Novel by

Cristina Comencini

Translated from the Italian
by Gregory Dowling

Pantheon Books   New York

All rights reserved under International and Pan-American Copyright
Conventions. Published in the United States by Pantheon Books, a
division of Random House, Inc., New York. Originally published in
Great Britain by Chatto & Windus Limited, London

Library of Congress Cataloging-in-Publication Data
Comencini. Cristina.
[Pagine strappate.   English]
The missing pages : a novel / Cristina Comencini.
p.   cm.
Translated from the Italian by Gregory Dowling. Cf. CIP front matter
ISBN 0-679-43076-8
1. Fathers and daughters—Italy—Fiction.   I. Title.
PQ4863.0423P3413   1994
853′.914—dc20   93-31275

Manufactured in the United States of America
First American Edition
9   8   7   6   5   4   3   2   1

Part 1

One

H e acknowledged the porters with a nod. The car door was opened for him and he stepped out into the courtyard which throbbed with the din from the street.

In the lift there was silence once again. As he made his way down the long corridor several people greeted him and he replied briskly. He found his secretary already hard at work, typing, and felt cheered by her efficiency.

'Call Migliani for me, please. Then Bosio. Don't put any calls through to me if you can avoid it.'

He entered his room, alone once more, and glanced through his correspondence. Thank heaven for these morning hours, when most of his employees had still to arrive, and he could concentrate on the day's dead-lines and all the documents that needed re-examining and signing. Later he would set the internal lines buzzing with messages, summonses, orders. But during those first few hours of the day he was the thinking head of an organism still dazed with sleep. The long windows had dark green curtains that blocked out light and movement. He sat in his comfortable leather armchair; the table in front of him was stacked with fresh newspapers, and a strong odour of wood and dust-coated documents hung over the room.

Guido Forte was sixty years old. He was one of those men who become good-looking as they get older. As a young man he had never liked the infantile cast of his face, his turned-up nose, his over-regular features. Now he had the style and tone of a man who had made it. But he gave no thought to this.

He lit a cigarette. He really should give it up. Everybody else was doing so. He picked up a paper and his eyes flickered over the headlines. Then he went straight to the business pages. He was looking for an item concerning himself. There it was, in a tiny column at the bottom of a page: just a brief summary of his speech at the conference. He wasn't happy with that. He'd made a perfect speech, elegant and stylishly composed, and it had been applauded. But it was a waste of time, paper and words. It was time he gave up going to conferences and making well-written, useless speeches.

'It's not important really,' he said to himself, but all the same he was annoyed at how little prominence the paper had given it.

He picked up another paper.

Guido Forte was honest, a skilled speaker and writer, and very good at his job. He was so capable that when he left off talking to people, they often found themselves floundering for words, wondering what to add, their minds inexplicably blank.

He had few friends. It was a fault, but it hardly bothered him. He had led a satisfying and successful life. His wife had given order and tranquillity to that side of his life which he was unable to cultivate owing to lack of time.

There was a knock at the door. Without waiting for an answer, an elderly man came in, dressed in a sober dark suit and a tie that was almost black. Forte greeted him, waved him to a chair, then remained silent for a few seconds as if waiting for something. The silence made the man visibly tense. Suddenly Forte started to talk. He asked how the other man was and then, without giving him time to reply, went straight to the point.

'As you know, Migliani, the board of directors is meeting in a fortnight's time.'

In a few words he explained the trouble they were in and why he had decided to entrust him with such an important task.

He summed up the aims of the other man's duties so concisely that Migliani felt as if he were watching himself at work.

'In a few days' time I'd like you to present me with a project that we can talk over,' he concluded.

Migliani nodded without thinking. The phone rang and Forte answered. Migliani's mind started to work.

'So,' Forte said, putting the phone down, 'just get a draft ready and we can start work on it together.'

'Yes, but . . .' Migliani hesitated, 'I have to see about reorganising my office. You remember, we've already discussed it.'

The phone rang again.

'Yes, I remember. But in the meantime think about what we're going to say when the board meets. Then we'll decide.' He made an irritated gesture towards the phone. 'I'm sorry, but this morning I can't get a moment's peace.'

He took the call at once, giving the other man no time to answer. Migliani went towards the door, dissatisfied and confused. It was only when he was in the corridor that he realised how menacingly close the deadline was that he had accepted so unthinkingly. He at once gave up the idea of the coffee he'd been looking forward to. When he got to his office he rang all his staff, one after the other, and then summoned his closest collaborator. He brought the deadline for the job forward and told him nothing of what lay behind the important task that their sector had been entrusted with.

Nobody in the institute's offices knew what went on on the other floors. There were rumours, people kept their eyes and ears open and tried to glean what information they could. But nobody could claim to be well-informed. The brighter employees invented complicated techniques by which they managed to read confidential documents upside-down on their bosses' desks and they exchanged all little items they picked up in this manner. New employees could never understand the reason for the invariably evasive replies they received, could never decipher the secret code by which – so it was generally believed – every statement of a superior was linked to a web of invisible intentions. This condition of amazement and diffidence never lasted long. Every day the new employee would receive so many warnings and precepts – seldom friendly ones – that he or she soon acquired the ability to react. Most adopted an attitude of mingled animosity and veneration towards those controlling the game from on high. The more uninterested ones simply took it for granted that power was a matter of obscure, fortuitous and at the same time cohesive forces which they could never hope to comprehend. There was always some part of the mechanism that eluded them; no explanation did justice to its complexity and adaptability. They had no means of access to the principle by which everything moved.

Bosio had been a great imitator ever since childhood. He had imitated the other children's handwriting at school, and now he imitated the clothes or the manner of speech of people he thought superior. He often imitated just for the pleasure of imitating. He had become so skilful at observing other people's behaviour that he could divine things that had never been said and was able to please anyone. But he needed to be faced by a strong personality, so that his shafts of acumen had something to bounce off. When he came up against a shy person, he crumbled. He avoided shy people like the plague.

For some years now he had been Forte's right-hand man.

He was now walking along the corridor of the

institute, towards his boss's room, preparing himself for his morning interview.

He tapped at the door and strode purposefully in. As usual he found Forte on the phone. He sat down comfortably in front of him, listening to the conversation without embarrassment.

'You're here at last. Good,' Forte began. 'We really can't afford to waste these first few hours of the morning.'

Bosio smiled familiarly. 'I've read the papers. Congratulations!' he said.

'Yes, they've given it some coverage,' Forte said dismissively, as if it mattered very little to him. 'Speeches, speeches!' he sighed, and changed the subject immediately. 'Last night we didn't discuss the financial side of the project. This morning I've spoken to the minister. He's given us carte blanche.'

Bosio smiled again before speaking. 'So all we have to do now is set about reorganising the design and projects office. I wrote a memo about it. Do you remember?'

'Design and projects. You mean Migliani. You've been wanting him out of the way for some time now, eh?'

They both smiled.

'We'll see,' Forte said, gazing at him ironically. 'Drop in around seven. We'll lock ourselves in and work on it. No, just a moment. I was forgetting. It's my daughter's birthday. I can't keep the family waiting too long. Come round at six.'

Bosio stood up and looked at Forte jauntily.

'Migliani looked worried. I met him in the corridor. Your interview must have shaken him. I don't think we should make him work too hard, he's not used to it.'

'So you don't know what I said to him, but you know I've seen him. Word gets around . . .'

The phone rang.

'I'll see you later.'

Forte watched him leave, pleased that he had told him nothing too precise.

'This craving of his to know everything,' he thought. 'It's too much.'

The phone continued to ring by his side.

'I really must remember to ask Marta what she's bought Silvia. I should at least know what I'm giving her. Yes, I suppose they did give my speech some coverage after all.'

He lifted the receiver.

Two

They had eaten very little. That evening there was to be a special dinner for her sister's birthday. Over lunch Federica had listened to her mother describing the list of food to be prepared. She imagined the bustle of people, the door-bell ringing, the shattered peace.

Now she lay on her bed, allowing herself a short break before returning to her studies. She held her legs upright, pointing straight to the ceiling, with a cushion balanced on the soles of her feet. She had often lain on her sister's feet in that same position. She recalled how the blood ran to her face as she held her hands out towards her sister, while they both laughed and swayed with the effort. They had done it hundreds of times. Kid's stuff, all in the past. She sent the cushion flying.

She picked up the book from the bedside table. She tried to fight off her after-lunch sleepiness. In one glance her eyes took in a whole page of the book, all forty-three lines of it. How long was it since she had managed to compose an entire sentence, to conclude a thought? When had she last talked? Outside, with other people, she got by with mono-syllables. In the house everybody talked and talked. Even the books talked. They were scored on every page with the whole family's underlinings. She had never read a wholly new book. So whenever she marked some untouched sentence, she didn't do so through choice but because its virgin state attracted her. If she ever felt like agreeing with some thought that had already been underlined, she was restrained by a curious sense of contamination. And her greatest concern was to remain undefiled by other people's thoughts.

She looked at the panel of photos above the desk. She sought the meaning of those underlined sentences in the girls' smiling faces. What had they been like then? There was too great an age gap between her and her sisters. She tried to understand them by pondering on the books and the markings. Or at least to create a difference between herself and them, so that she wouldn't follow in other people's footsteps – footsteps that had gone astray, completely astray. The gulf that separated her from her sisters could never be bridged. Caterina and Silvia: no doubt each of them had had her moment of rebellion. They had certainly debated and argued. They had sent objects flying and then stuck them together again and put them back in their places. But she loved those objects just as they were: antiquated and useless; nothing in the world would ever induce her to dispute where they were placed, or discuss possible alternatives. The world must be taken just as it was. It must be left in peace.

She stared out of the window at the cloudy sky. She thought once again of the journey she had long dreamt of taking. She imagined herself with just a strip of cotton for a skirt, her hair in plaits, and her skin tanned a rich dark-brown, sitting in a field of red earth and mud, surrounded by naked children and busy mothers. She couldn't have explained that uncontaminated dream to anyone. She knew every possible answer. As usual she had no counter-argument to put forward. It was true: every dream of escape is essentially childish; the real condition of those people she dreamt of was hunger and poverty; the journey to virgin lands was merely an ancient and decadent myth. But the dream was invincible, it survived all such cerebral observations. And she continued to cultivate it and to love it, just as she loved her noiseless room and the books in which she sought the key to those faces on her wall.

She thought of the books open on her desk. She should get down to her studies again. It had been a mistake to take up philosophy at the university. Every time she had an exam to take, books began to amass on her table. Every single statement, every idea sent her scurrying to another book, to another sentence she'd read God knows where. She proceeded by a series of intuitions, jotting down pages of hap-hazard quotations. She felt a continual need to re-establish the basics and she despised the way the other students worked. In all the lectures she'd attended so far, she hadn't yet come across one fellow student who was capable of independent thought. The first thing she did, when getting to grips with the subject of each exam, was to go into her father's study and pull out several volumes. She would start reading them and get lost in the notes and references. She would sit there on the floor by the bookcase for hours at a time, surrounded by books. Her eyes would jump from one text to another, seeking that chance encounter that would resolve her problem: a succinct truth that would bear up under all that mass of knowledge. But each time things merely became more and more complicated and she would lose her way in a labyrinth of imprecise contradictions. At times she had a sense of herself as a person with a particular skill for picking up signs that had been overlooked by other people, and then, a minute later, she was no more than a mind crushed by uncertainty and confusion.

She would go out for a walk, and when she came back, she would put all the books back, empty her drawers and clear her desk. On the table she would just leave her notes and the sentences she'd collected. And when her desk was clutter-free again, and the tottering piles of books had been removed, she would concentrate everything she had learnt into one polished sentence. She would copy it out on to a clean sheet of paper and her mind would fill with scorn for the useless tangles of erudition, for the game she had not allowed herself to get involved in.

Currently she was in a phase of purity and rigour.

There were only two books on the desk, and a sheet of paper on which she'd written the title of an essay she intended to put forward to the professor. The title seemed so perfect that she had been unable to add to it.

She forced herself to sit at the table and stared hard at the title. Then she started writing:

> The fundamental problem of our age is to know whether it is possible to make goodness beautiful. Why ask this question? There is no doubt that the concept of virtue is in steep decline. For a religious person there is some sense in being virtuous and good, since in that case it's a law that must be obeyed and the law carries its own reward: the fact of belonging to an institutional, moral and intellectual order. But how can the person with no religious sense be stirred to goodness?

She heard footsteps in the corridor. Her mother's footsteps. The door opened. Her mother stood there, holding two tablecloths.

'Which one should I use? You might give me a hand.'

Federica turned slowly. 'What time are they coming?'

'Eight o'clock, but what's that got to do with it? We have to get ready.'

Federica looked at the two tablecloths: one was white and embroidered; the other pink and plain.

She realised that her mother was asking her what tone to give to the evening.

'The white one's too good,' she answered. 'There's no reason to use that. It's just us, isn't it?'

'Too good? Why? It's ages since we were all here together.'

So that was how it was. Her mother was set upon the notion of a white, matrimonial-type celebration. Federica gazed at her mother, whose face was as white and transparent as the cloth. Nothing ever made her cross. Everything about her was distant and elusive. Her eyes always held the faded glimmer of an original intuition. To Federica she appeared remote and worthy of respect.

'You're right, put the white one on. But you don't need me. You don't need to do anything, the daily does it all.'

'You know that that's not true, but it doesn't matter.'

She closed the door again. Federica listened to her footsteps receding down the corridor. She returned to her essay.

Three

———

He turned the light on over the table. At last he could work. His secretary had gone, and so had most of the staff. Forte glanced out of the window. The curtains were now open and let in the darkness of the evening, the car headlights and the distant rumble of engines. It was an hour he liked: the evening, when the only sound in the empty offices was the clattering of the cleaning-ladies' buckets. It was the pleasure of the monk in his cloisters.

He opened the file on his desk and drew out some typewritten sheets. Bosio's paper. He read it quickly; he underlined a few sentences and jotted some comments in the margin. Five pages to make one point: the design and projects office doesn't work, isn't integrated with the rest of the firm, produces waste-paper, eliminate. Eliminate Migliani.

'Compared with the usual stuff,' he thought, 'he's been concise. He wants the design and projects office closed and each sector to do its own research. Correct or false, it depends. It's an idea: the research a firm does is either operational or of no use; academic studies are a university's province. There's just as much to be said on the opposite side: a company like ours, with the funds it handles, needs an office that specialises in study and research. Bosio must have had problems with studying when he was young. There's some kind of complex at the root of his attitude. We'll have to find a compromise. For the moment we can shift a few duties around and wait. The design and projects office will stay.'

He wrote 'to be discussed' at the end of the document and passed on to the next paper. He read another memo. Here the problem was more intricate though the question was basically the same: company efficiency in a public enterprise. He looked up and stared at the bare wall.

'Everything is possible. There's no such thing as a wrong or right position. What's important is to recognise the individual criteria that determine a particular choice.'

Forte's mind turned to the colleague he'd been talking to a few minutes earlier. Bosio was intelligent. He was one of the few who'd understood that there was nothing to understand. Most young people start a new job by trying to grasp the concepts that govern it, and seek to apply their knowledge. But Bosio had realised at once that it was all a matter of organisation and psychology. At times Forte had the feeling that he was thinking with two brains, his own and Bosio's. He was irritated by the way Bosio picked up his thoughts so perfectly and so swiftly, the way he anticipated them and acted upon them like a faithful wife. But he had to acknowledge the man's skill.

Thinking back over his own career, he realised that there had been a moment when his own concept of work had undergone a radical change. That moment had coincided with an acceleration of his powers of command. It had all happened within the space of a few months.

It was spring, and he had just turned forty. He was stubbornly pursuing a confused and elusive project aimed at affirming himself. In the evenings he would go to sleep convinced that the goal was close at hand but oppressed by a sense of mental disorder that prevented him from attaining his aims. It was all his own fault, but he argued frequently with his wife over financial worries and over the lack of system and silence in the house. At night he would retire to his study, and sit smoking with the persistence of an insomniac. It was at this time that Federica, his youngest daughter, was born.

It was then, too, that he had become fascinated by the committed attitude of a woman who had just started work at the office. For weeks he had observed her unflustered movements and the indefinable remoteness of her eyes. In this way he had distracted himself from his feelings of defeat. For three months he left the office at the same time as all the rest of the staff. At that hour it was still light. He visited the tourist sights of the city with the taciturn girl. He savoured the pleasure of lies. When he started serious work again, and looked at the baby for the first time, he realised he had lost for ever all his convictions about work, but he felt strangely free and sure of himself. Just after university, he had found a job collecting statistics. He had been paid by the day to get people to fill up forms, to interview them and add up answers. At the time he had imagined that each cross in a little box and each cyphered assessment of a company constituted data that would help other people to make proposals and take decisions. But in fact it was the question that supplied the answer; and the firms disappeared or multiplied according to the categories that were used to group them, the research that had to be carried out, or the thesis that one wanted to demonstrate.

No logical premise existed by which it could be decided who was right and who was wrong. No system had any greater validity than that consequent on a few hypotheses. That was all there was to it. Everything depended on how an idea was put forward, on the certainty with which one pretended to support it. There was no point in wasting time debating with oneself. Facts and decisions were the fruit of coincidences or of contrasts with other ideas and opinions that were all equally coherent. There were always innumerable alternatives, and it was all a question of assessing people's tones and working out the various sides they were on. Most people were looking for some definitive truth to enshrine in a display-case. They merely confused issues and, in the end, they never understood who had decided the rules of the game.

Somewhere in his bookcase, he had preserved a photograph of the woman he had gone out with, but he had forgotten all about her.

In his youngest daughter's serious face, Forte recognised the anxiety of those months; and, at the same time, something of his own attitude towards youth. She had been born during a turbulent period of his life and thus his relationship with her was somewhat different from the attitude of tender indifference he had towards his other daughters. He met her eyes with fear and emotion.

Four

———

They were lounging at ease on the sofas, having finished dinner. The conversation proceeded in short bursts, with fragmentary remarks and interruptions. Caterina, Forte's second daughter, spoke up. She had in fact been talking for the last minute or two to her sister. Now she raised her voice, to let everyone know the subject of their conversation.

'People work in different ways. For instance, how long are you out of the house each day?' she asked her sister's husband. 'At least ten hours, I'll bet. OK, you're needed at the office, but suppose she were to do the same?' She indicated her sister again.

Silvia's husband interrupted her at once. 'I just think that if two people aren't prepared to make a few sacrifices, they shouldn't have children.'

He looked at his sister-in-law provocatively. There had always been a good-natured antipathy between the two of them which brought them into constant collision. Their two partners said nothing, each eyeing their respective spokesperson protectively.

'So if you've got children, one of the two has

to work less, is that it?' Caterina insisted, observing him ironically. 'Either one? It makes no difference?'

'All right, Caterina, I know what you're trying to say, but ideologically it's a stupid position . . .' He faltered momentarily and then said with new confidence: 'Lots of men choose to work less.'

Caterina was losing her patience. She was irritated by her sister's silence and by the way she looked so compliantly at her husband. Caterina preferred her brother-in-law; at least there was something going on inside his head. She wanted to torment her sister, to spur her into a reaction. Silvia sat there so serenely, a picture of placidity and satisfaction. She had three children, she worked eight hours a day and everything was all right in her life. Apparently. How did she manage it?

Caterina looked at her own husband. He was watching her as well, and smiling. Her problems with her children, her qualms over the hours she should devote to them, were all resolved by self-sacrifice on her part, which made things very easy for him. The only way to wipe that smile off his face would be for her to disappear for days at a time and to let everything get out of hand – but she could never bring herself to do that.

Now they were all talking together. Their voices cut in on one another and none of them managed to complete a sentence.

Federica kept silent, looking through a book. Forte looked at his two elder daughters. Occasionally he nodded as they spoke. He noticed that there was something in their eyes that made them identical. As children they had had thin arms and long, bird-like legs. He recalled that old gawkiness with melancholy.

'Girls don't stay slim and silent for long,' he thought.

The image of a boy with short hair and big silent eyes floated up from the memory of a distant desire. He looked at Federica; in her place he saw a dark-haired boy sitting cross-legged, with strong shoulders and a firm straight back. Federica lifted her long black hair on to her shoulder. Forte re-focused on his youngest daughter.

'She's different from the other two,' he thought. 'Prouder, quieter.'

But he didn't know whether this was a good or a bad thing. Probably the best one could wish for her was that she would turn out normal like the other two, experience their conflicts, and find a man to sleep with. At times there flickered before him the possibility of a free existence, unconditioned and uncontrolled by outside forces, but then he at once feared that such mirages could only lead to unhappiness for her. He worried, too, over the time she wasted at the university and her inability to go out with the same person for more than three evenings.

Fragments of the discussion reached him and he shook these thoughts off. The topic had changed without anybody realising it. Forte spoke up and there was a moment of silence.

'You're putting the question in the wrong terms. The years since the war have helped us to reconstruct a sense of normality in society, after all that endless killing. If it hadn't been for the war, we would have gone on in the same way. There wouldn't have been the need for discussion. We've had to rediscover certain obvious ideas. When you're surrounded by the destruction caused by war, you have to use your brains. We think we have been so creative, but in fact we have done nothing new since the war.'

He fell silent. He knew the chorus of opposition this would stir up. One of his know-all daughters was already answering him.

'But why does she go on reading that book?' he thought, observing Federica's indifference. 'Is she really so uninterested in what I say?'

'You talk about the war as if it was just an unfortunate accident,' Silvia said to her father, 'an unexpected leap backwards, a waste of time. What do you mean by that?'

Forte leaned forward to see the cover of the book that Federica continued to read; he felt like taking it from her. He answered Silvia's question patiently but with some vexation.

'I believe that at every historic moment there are various possible futures. Obviously it's not only chance that determines them, there must be a historical conjuncture. But all the same, chance is a deciding factor. Chance and individual choices.'

He broke off because he knew they hadn't understood him.

'Anyway,' he concluded, 'maybe you're right. It's ages since I've thought about these things.'

Federica looked up; she scrutinised her father without saying a word. Forte went inexplicably red. He tried to engage her, but Federica had already lowered her eyes again. He felt hurt by her silence.

'There must be some way to get her to join in,' he thought; the conversation had already passed on to daily politics; he picked up occasional remarks and it struck him it was just like being at the office. He said no more all evening.

Exactly one month after that dinner, Forte started to jot down his thoughts in a notebook, as he had done during that distant period of infidelity.

He wrote:

> Federica isn't talking. I realised it for the first time on the evening of Silvia's birthday. Then I thought it was just a way of keeping out of our usual family chat. But now I realise there's something I'm unable to grasp. She keeps silent deliberately and this decision of hers, which we can't understand, seems to set her above us. When we ask her a question, she always finds the shortest answer, just so that nobody can say anything more to her. Marta is worried too. Whenever we have a meal together, we keep waiting anxiously for her to say something. We do all we can to encourage her to talk. Even if she comes out with something totally trivial, we greet it like a great revelation. Yesterday I asked her straight out why she never joins in. She said it was just that every time she begins a sentence, she feels like starting it again. She

asked me if she could write notes to me in the evening. I remember she used to do that as a child. She said that when you write you can talk without being interrupted. Maybe we shouldn't worry too much. It'll pass. She took her exam and got full marks. She reads, she writes, she leads a normal life. I haven't written what I think for nineteen years — Federica's age.

Five

_____

Caterina was lying on the bed in Federica's room. She had had lunch with her mother and her sister. Then her mother had retired to her room for a rest and Federica had gone out. The meal had been a nightmare. In an effort to lighten the atmosphere, Caterina had talked about her children, recalling episodes from their infancy. She had tried to break her sister's silence. Her mother had summoned her for that purpose, but it had all been useless.

Everything was quiet now. The grandfather clock in the hall echoed hollowly. There was nothing provisional about this house. The objects were all unremovable. Outside there was plenty of light, but the house would have none of it. The windows were double-glazed, and the trees in the park opposite were framed as in a picture. There were several pictures hanging on the walls, all signed with famous names.

Caterina had been wandering from one room to another. The room she once slept and studied in was now a wardrobe. She lingered in her father's study but there were too many books there: it was impossible to pick one out and read it. She went into her sister's room, which had something of all their rooms within it. The bed, the desk and the bedside table were hers. The bookcase was Silvia's. Federica had picked and rejected other people's furniture and thus created a bedroom that could only have been hers. Passionate care had gone into composing a mysteriously meticulous whole. The curtains and bedcover were Indian. They were the only splashes of colour; the rest of the room was Swiss in its whiteness and coolness. There were just a few posters on the wall, all of which were unusual and of high quality. There was nothing banal, no student's bric-à-brac or junk. The table held an exercise-book and a white marble egg. This was the only room in which Federica had left any traces of herself; elsewhere she remained silent; she passed light-footed, avoiding objects and people.

Everything was stripped to its essence and old-fashioned. Caterina's old desk now exhaled a maniacal purity. There was a smell of sharpened pencils, of ink, of clean sheets and scrubbed floor-tiles: it was the bedroom of a small child or an institution.

Slips of paper protruded from the exercise-book. Caterina read: 'ideas and notes to write to him'; 'essay on virtue'; 'nonsense from home and outside'. This last title aroused her curiosity; she opened the exercise-book and read at random:

> There's just no nobility in their words. They're so stupid! They're selling their own lives. They've got no pride, just cheap psycho-mumble.

Caterina lit a cigarette and sat at the desk. She looked up at the panel of photos and observed Federica as a child with her hair in plaits, her hands over her mouth, her eyes gleaming and ironic. She read on:

> Silvia's self-satisfied, nothing can shake her. Maybe nothing ever *has* shaken her. She's an empty vessel. At least she's not irritating. But as for Caterina! Trying so hard to claw her way up to other people's level, to understand them, to map out everybody's designs. Caterina is the exact opposite of everything I love. So touchingly sensitive, with tears on tap, trusting in the power of words. She thinks she's real, sincere. Every word she utters is a banal generalisation. How could I have loved her so much as a girl?

Caterina put a hand to her heart. It was beating rapidly and violently. She felt as if she were staring at herself in a mirror wearing a stupid vulgar mask. Could she really be as banal as her sister thought? She wanted to close the exercise-book. She had always believed that if you read things surreptitiously, you were the one to suffer: the knowledge you gained was false. But the opening of the next sentence drew her too strongly:

> Mamma hides her feelings and pretends to be busy with little things. Maybe she isn't worth much either, but I can't judge her. When she

29

walks through the rooms and closes the windows so gracefully, when she passes so lightly down the corridor, I listen to her through the door and think that without her this perfect little place of mine wouldn't exist either. Today she came looking for me. She came into my room and sat knitting while I studied. I know she loves me best; more than Silvia and Caterina who are always asking her for things. More than Papà who's never here. It's my silence she loves above all. She pretends to be worried, but actually she approves of it, she thinks it's like her own. She couldn't be more wrong! There's an abyss between me and her, and her love makes me angry.

Caterina flipped through the closely-written pages. She stopped at a half-empty one. There was just a single block of writing in the middle:

I love old people and children because they're the only ones who play. Everyone else, all those who are half-way between, all those who believe blindly in their thoughts and their actions, horrify me. Papà said to me once: you should read with a sense of detachment, and always be aware that what you write yourself may be as valuable as what the book says. Don't pay too much attention to the things they teach you. I'd like to unmask him. I will one day.

Caterina closed the exercise-book. She couldn't go

on. There was just one question in her mind: who was she?

She got up from the chair and felt her hands and legs trembling. She went into the bathroom and looked dazedly at herself in the mirror.

'Why doesn't she talk to us? What's happened? Where is she now?'

She went quietly into the room where her mother lay with her cheek resting on her arm; she appeared to be having no more than a nap. The whole room was shuttered and the curtains let no light in. There wasn't a wrinkle on the bed. Her mother's body looked as if it had been placed there by somebody else.

'Does she realise?'

She felt tender towards her mother and also inexplicably guilty.

'Why is she sleeping like that? Why is she so pale? Why is this room like this? Why have I never noticed before?'

The only noise was her mother's breathing. Her lips were closed. Caterina wanted to wake her. She approached, but Federica's words came back to mind. On the bedside table there were photos of all three of them.

She left the room. She tiptoed down the corridor and got her coat. The clock's ticking in the hall was more oppressive than ever. The objects that had seemed so perfectly in place were now wandering aimlessly in space. The profound relations between things were all lost. Her mother was sleeping in the end room, a long way off. The living-room looked like the façade of a chapel.

She left the house. She closed the door and ran down the steps. From the street, the rows of windows resumed their reassuring appearance.

'I'm too emotional – Federica's right. Nothing's changed. I used to keep a diary too but I was always afraid that someone might find it. Mamma – I mustn't leave her on her own. If she wakes up, she'll be scared. I'll go back and take her some coffee.'

Six

—————

Federica was talking less and less. She had with-drawn into the shell of herself and hardly ever left her room. She wrote messages to her father. Every morning, before going to the office, Forte would leave his reply on the table by the bed where his daughter lay asleep.

Federica was aware of the growing influence of her messages on her father. He, who never listened to anyone and trusted only himself, now awaited her letters anxiously. Federica took advantage of it. She would let two or three evenings go by without writing anything; she would wait and then send him a letter full of remarks that had often been copied from books and which contained just an occasional hint of her affection. Forte would then be happier than he had been for ages. Federica conceded herself drop by drop. Every so often she would ram the cork in tightly, and Forte would have to face her irre-vocable silence just like everybody else. Then, when the letters turned up again, close-written and dense, his fear would turn to complicity and pride.

'She's really intelligent!' he thought. 'So strong and thoughtful. Freer and more intelligent than the others.'

These thoughts would pass through his mind in the morning, as he felt the letter in his jacket pocket and looked forward to reading it in his office at leisure. On other occasions, faced with his daughter's silence, her unconnecting eyes, the superior air with which she maintained a stubborn silence or answered in monosyllables, a sudden fear would grip him. He wrote in his notebook:

> Marta wants to consult a doctor. Federica isn't well. It's not natural at her age to stay in her room for hours in silence. The letters she writes to me are so full of ideas that I don't know how she can have thought all these things at her age. One day she says one thing, and the next day she rejects it. She can write two contradictory sentences one after the other, but one doesn't realise at first because they both seem to be in tune with some personal position of hers, which still eludes me. What she writes is both highly intelligent and completely unpredictable. After all, it's not so very strange to remain silent. When she wants to she talks. Every so often I get the impression she's making fun of me. I'm plagued by a feeling of anxiety that I can't attribute to anything specific. It's as if she were walking along a high-wire and every so often pretending to fall. I suffer from sudden

attacks of rapid heart-beats and I'm constantly aware of my body. She's got a will of iron. She seems to want to test herself and me. Sometimes I'm afraid to write to her, to encourage her muteness in this way. Maybe I'll have to talk to someone about it.

But in the morning, as he read his daughter's latest letter in the car, he felt less anxious. He dismissed his wife's worries as unfounded.

Forte had a great respect for every thinking being, even a child. He had observed his daughters as they grew up, all the while keeping his own counsel; he was afraid of conditioning them, of hindering their free development. It was impossible for him to consider a child as a creature in need of laws. He was convinced that the rules given to children only served to make adults feel secure, since they were incapable of living their own lives, incapable of freedom.

He had had little success with Caterina and Silvia. They had always been closer to their mother. They had rebelled against minor prohibitions; they had engaged in politics a little, at a time when all young people took an interest in them, but it had led them nowhere. They got married. They gave up their studies, started their little jobs – like so many women.

With Federica it had been different. He had not had much time to devote to his daughters, but for her he had put aside half an hour every evening before she went to bed.

He used to take her into his study and together

they organised games of skill, they read books and chatted. He started by sitting her up on his table before she could even walk. He took wooden blocks from a bag and she had to drop them into a cube by finding the right-shaped aperture. It was an old family game. The other two daughters had played it as well. But with Federica each game was different, each game became something new. She would challenge him and then observe his movements in silence, an expression of fierce concentration on her face. Then she would repeat them with ease, adding something of her own. He watched her in amazement, proud of her cleverness.

They never hugged. Forte was embarrassed by gestures of affection. Federica didn't seem to seek signs of tenderness from him.

As she grew up, Federica asked him about the office and his life outside. She told him what she thought and almost advised him. When there was some new game to play together, and Forte started to read out the instructions, she would interrupt him, examine the pieces in the box and invent new rules. He had kept all the boxes in a cupboard in the study, even though none of them contained the original game. Federica used to mix the pieces up and alter the routes they were supposed to follow. They had overturned the logic of Snakes and Ladders: instead of following the route mapped out towards the final goal, you had to go as slowly as possible, trying not to get there first, lingering delightfully in the traps and snares along the way. Real luck was falling down a 'snake' and getting sent back, and then watching the other player move forward inexorably towards that final square, where victory was transformed into defeat.

But then those rules had to be changed too; nothing was ever allowed to become boring or habitual. Forte and his daughter would modify them even as they played; sometimes, when the game was apparently over, they would reinforce the old penalties and prizes. Occasionally the confusion between old and new rules, between the various and contradictory goals to be achieved, made it impossible to decide what was admissible as a move.

Forte enjoyed himself and, feeling proud of his clever daughter, he would gently stroke her cheek. Federica would then shift away, not letting him touch her; she would stare gravely at him. Her eyes held a silent reproach for something that Forte didn't understand. Before he could make it out, Federica would either disappear into her room or change the subject.

As she grew up, these evening encounters became rarer but never ceased altogether. Forte loved to listen to his daughter. Federica didn't trust other people's opinions; she always tried to gather sufficient data to reach her own conclusions. Forte didn't know how far she was influenced in this by his own example; he had never revealed his thoughts to her or to anybody. Yet he was sure that Federica was moving in the same direction – without any hesitation, without his fears and his disappointments.

But now she no longer spoke to him. In the

executive car that took him to the office, Forte delved into his memories, seeking the reasons for this silence, for these strange and totally unexpected manifestations of hostility. And he could not bring himself to consult a doctor about the problem.

'What would a doctor know about it?' he thought. 'This isn't a medical question. It's something else. You just have to look at what she writes.'

And he comforted himself by reading his daughter's letters, arguing to himself that only intelligent, highly intelligent, people are able to perceive the real difficulties that life presents.

'There is nothing the matter with my daughter,' he thought.

Seven

Forte now dressed with more care than usual. He had never been particularly elegant. He always used the same aftershave, wore the same type of shirts and ties. But recently he had begun to feel unsure of himself. He was uneasy about his appearance, insecure of what he said or wrote in his notes. He pondered longer than usual over every decision that needed taking.

Bosio observed him. He had always measured his boss's superiority by the ease with which he worked, by his complete lack of strain or exaggerated commitment. Now Forte was slipping. Bosio didn't know why and was eager to find out. Forte hadn't told anybody about his daughter. He had no true friends he could consult.

They were sitting opposite each other in Forte's room. Bosio was talking, illustrating the financial implications of his reorganisation plan. His voice was punctilious and unhesitating. Forte followed the movements of his hands, observed the complacent expression with which he displayed his powers of concision and acuteness.

'He's quite a phenomenon,' he couldn't help thinking. 'If I'd asked him to study the financial advantages of an air-raid, he'd use the same terms. He'd never mention the word "bomb" or "corpse", but he'd say, "By carefully classifying all the relevant categories of costs and benefits and making a simultaneous quantitative analysis of those items that can reasonably be quantified, it is possible to provide a solid basis on the grounds of which a final decision might eventually be reached".'

Bosio had finished. He was waiting to be praised. Forte said nothing and made him suffer for a while.

'He's learnt a great deal here with me,' he thought, studying him. 'When he's in my job, if he ever gets there, he'll have to decide between the various combinations of "final decisions". Let's see if he's mature enough to take my place.'

'Fine,' said Forte after a long silence. 'So we close the section run by Migliani and give the major research projects to outside companies.'

Forte paused to collect his thoughts.

'I'm thinking, yes. Yes. I asked Migliani to put in a report on the same issue.'

Bosio's face muscles tightened imperceptibly.

Forte picked up a bound typescript. He opened it and flipped randomly through its pages, stopping at a sentence here and there.

'A brilliant study,' he went on. 'Like yours. Persuasive data and assessments. Reaching conclusions diametrically opposed to yours. Yet valid.'

'What do you mean, valid?' Bosio interrupted. 'We've

talked it through several times. Migliani's position is hopelessly out of date. And anyway he's far too closely involved to be able to make a clear assessment.'

'It's worth considering, I assure you. His assessment is reasoned and to the point, just like yours. Now . . . would you like a cigarette?'

'No, thank you,' Bosio answered brusquely.

'Now . . .' Forte sighed, flicking the lighter, 'I'd like some advice. We've talked about it several times.'

'Migliani's standing up for himself,' Bosio interrupted again, 'it's natural. But listen, we have to face facts and restructure his section. And now we've actually got the means to do it.'

'I know,' Forte smiled, continuing to leaf through Migliani's document. 'But reading this . . . yes, let's say he's almost convinced me. He's an intelligent man, Migliani, you know.'

Bosio looked at him disconcertedly, unable to read his boss's thoughts.

'The design office, in a way, has worked perfectly well all these years,' Forte went on. 'Just for a moment, let's re-examine the whole question; let's take Migliani's opinion seriously too; he could be right.'

Here Forte looked up. Bosio turned red. He was in difficulties. Such a thing hadn't happened to him in ages. In amazement, Forte observed the transformation that his face was undergoing.

'Migliani runs the design office. He's obviously going to defend its role,' Bosio said hoarsely.

'He believes that it's important to maintain it,' Forte stated, looking him straight in the eyes.

'Of course . . .' stammered Bosio. 'We know that. He's been clinging onto his own special line for ages. He won't accept any innovations, new principles, the principle of elasticity . . .'

He couldn't go on. He suddenly realised how vague that idea was. It struck him that he'd never actually had to explain it. He didn't even know what the idea of elasticity consisted of. Fewer companies, fewer firms. Everyone talked about it. It was the right idea, Bosio thought. It fitted in with his impulse to get places, travelling as light as possible, unburdened by traditions. He himself had no traditions worth speaking of. So this principle suited him down to the ground. Everything connected with work should be neat and tidy, short and simple, cut and dried. New products, new processes. Above all, paper-free offices: as little paper as possible, and capacious waste-paper baskets. Speed, efficiency, readiness to move on to new matters. All the slogans and key-words were at his lips but just at that moment he couldn't exactly expound the principle of elasticity. The only clear definition that came to him was the opposite of Migliani; Migliani on one side of the fence and himself on the other.

'But Migliani won't accept that the rules have changed,' he said heatedly; there were no gaps in his knowledge of Migliani's faults. 'He's never had any sense of the company as a whole. The design office has never produced anything of any concrete use. You've often said so yourself' – and he looked at his boss, expecting at least a nod. But Forte wasn't looking at him, he was observing a distant point on the wall. 'You know what Migliani's like. When he has to present a study, he's fine, a perfectionist. There won't be a single mistake in the typing or the figures. But who reads it? Who ever reads a single line of it? Nobody. And what use is it? But the professor had to do it. And look at all his ideas!'

'Migliani has a lot of ideas then?' Forte interrupted him, suddenly staring him in the eyes. 'So his position is clear, is it?'

'Yes,' quavered Bosio, 'in a certain sense. But wrong.'

'Right for him,' Forte insisted. 'Right from his point of view. And what's your position?'

'The advantage for the company in maintaining a design and projects office is minimal, as I was saying earlier, if we examine the costs . . .'

Forte interrupted him: 'Migliani talks about the advantage for the company as well.'

'Last year, at that conference, do you remember the speech we prepared together?' Bosio started again.

'Yes, of course I remember,' Forte said coldly.

'We said how important it was to link research to objectives, to concentrate on specialisation, on industrial research . . . We wrote . . . I think . . .' he stammered, 'I think in that article, just a second, I'm looking for the point, I quoted a passage in my paper here, hang on . . .'

He looked down and examined the sheaf of papers in his hands, his report. Everything had suddenly become confused and inexplicable. If Forte would only utter a single remark, even just the opening of a remark, he would at once sense what was wanted of him. As always. In all those years he had often dreaded a moment like this. Being taken unprepared, no papers to hand. Nobody knew his secret. He had always taken note of dates, deadlines, remarks and figures. He wasn't intelligent. He never had been. But he had put everything into seeming so. It was all a matter of learning things by heart, as at school, and pretending to understand them: the changes, the rules and the stratagems. Thus he had proved the most intelligent of all because nobody had ever rumbled him. He had taken them all in: those below him and those above. He had studied their every trick, their every move. Because there was no doubt about it: the others didn't have the same problem; they were brainier than he was. But he had got ahead, and they hadn't. And now he couldn't even find the point he was looking for. If only he could go to his own office and get his papers in order! He would at least be able to play for time. Time to think and look for the idea to put forward.

'What do you want from me? What's the right idea?'

'Bosio, don't look so worried. There's no right thing to say.'

Bosio looked at him incredulously. 'But that's not . . .' he stumbled.

'You've done a good piece of work,' Forte concluded. 'Leave the papers with me, I'll think it over. Now I've got other things to do. We'll talk about it some other time.'

'So I'll leave them with you, shall I?' said Bosio, standing up. His legs felt heavy. He knew that he'd gone red in the face and his hair was dishevelled. He put his hand up to cover the thinning spot. 'See you at three then,' he said as he walked out, his voice unsteady.

Forte gazed at the door as it closed. Bosio's insecurity had surprised him. He had never seen him in such a state. In all those years together, nothing like that had ever happened. Bosio was the only person he'd ever thought of as succeeding him. Good at writing. Quick in his calculations and financial assessments.

'What's he lacking?' he wondered.

He recalled little details and tricks he'd uncovered in their years of work together.

Once – just after Bosio had joined the company – Forte had caught him jotting down some remark of his in a little notepad, hidden under the desk. Some perfectly average remark. He'd asked him why was he taking a note of it. Bosio hadn't been able to answer.

On another occasion, Bosio had been ill. Forte had needed some papers from his office. His secretary had gone to Bosio's room to look for them. She had come back, saying that Bosio always locked away all his material in a cupboard before going home.

'He keeps everything in the cupboard,' his secretary said. 'Even his pens. And nobody's ever seen what's inside.'

Not long before, his secretary had told him something else. Bosio had invited her to dinner several times, and eventually she had accepted. Women didn't like Bosio; they treated him like a dangerous child. On this occasion the two of them had gone out to dinner and then back to Bosio's house for a drink.

His secretary had laughed as she spoke: 'His house looks like an office inside. Great heaps of documents, newspaper-cuttings. He subscribes to every magazine you can think of and keeps them all. On any subject.'

Forte had laughed at the time. But he paid no attention to gossip.

'Nice sort of chap, that Bosio,' he remembered Migliani saying. Migliani couldn't stand Bosio. 'For two weeks he's been buzzing round me, asking me for a copy of a report I've written. I've told him it's not ready yet, I'll give him a copy when it is, and not to worry. Yesterday the original disappeared. It was in a drawer in my desk. I asked him if he'd seen it. He said he hadn't but he had a funny look on his face as he said it. It didn't matter much; I'd already made copies. And anyway there was nothing secret in it. But do you think he's right in the head?'

Forte hadn't believed him. Migliani was getting old. He had probably left the document lying around somewhere.

On his way out Migliani had murmured, 'I reckon he's crazy.'

Forte picked up the paper-knife.

'Crazy, who knows. Maybe not. Just confused. Bosio's intelligent. A strange kind of intelligence. Poor chap. I'll try and talk to him later.'

He stared at the wall again. His mind was a confusion of contradictory thoughts. He opened a drawer and took out a folder from where it lay hidden under some documents. He pulled a letter out of the folder. He didn't read it; he knew it by heart. He observed the handwriting: it was still childish. She never used the same pen.

'She's still young,' he murmured.

He swallowed some saliva and looked up at the ceiling.

'What's happening to me? Maybe she's just confused as well. But this is a completely different matter. It's got nothing to do with the other one. I must keep my head and not get things muddled. I keep seeing resemblances in everything today. But it's not like that. It's easy to get confused.'

He looked at the letter and read:

'Thou dost preserve the stars from wrong; and the most ancient heavens, through Thee, are fresh and strong.' A beautiful poem. I found it in my book of Indian philosophy. When I finish university, I'll go abroad. You agree I should. You've always told me one should travel and see different things. Some distant place which I imagine as fresher and stronger, like the heavens in the poem. Larger than ours. The only thing I love in this city is my room. Outside everyone keeps talking, saying that this or that is right or wrong. I don't know what their grounds are. As for the journey, obviously I'd like you to come with me. And suppose we set off at once, without waiting? You see how important letters are. I'd never have dared to say this to you in words. Maybe if we do get away, I'll get better. Don't reply by listing your problems at work. Just say yes or no. But I'm not scared to stay in my room a little longer either. I'm not ill. There's no need to worry about me. Don't start plotting with Mamma, or with Caterina and Silvia. I trust you.

Forte closed the letter and looked at his watch. He rose and got his coat and hat. He suddenly felt old. He passed through to his secretary's room.

'I'm going out. You can tell people I'll be back in an hour.'

As he stood in the lift reserved for him and a few other members of staff he felt a sudden tremor.

'Guilty. Am I guilty of something? That woman, when Federica was born. Of course that would make it easier to understand. Marta suffered. Maybe it's the kind of thing you don't realise until later. Yes, it would all be easier to understand then and something could be done about it. I'll talk to Caterina. She's sensitive and she's got children. Maybe for once she'll be able to help me. Yes, I'll go and see her. At once.'

In the courtyard, the porter opened the car door for him. Forte didn't notice, went straight past the parked cars, and walked out in to the street.

Eight

L ong lines of cars rumbled down the street. Students and office-workers jostled their way along
the pavement past shop-assistants leaning against
their shutters. It was closing time for lunch. Forte dodged
his way through the crowds; he slipped into the narrow
corridors formed by the cars. Some of them braked
so close that the bottom of his coat swirled about
him and flapped in the fume-filled air against their
dead headlights. The day was cold, but the sky was
a summer blue just veiled by a distant white. The
sky itself seemed remote from the rooftops. Between
the tiles and the blue there was a hazy band of emp-
tiness: an insulation strip held in place by the aerials.

'What was her name? Her surname? God knows.
She had a cool neck and her cheek was deliciously
soft to the touch. She never used to say a word –
or maybe she talked, maybe she told me stories and
I just don't remember now. But I can recall every
detail of those walks: Portico d'Ottavia, Isola Tiberina,
Gianicolo; we went to Villa Adriana as well. The loveli-
est place of all. It was there, in the library courtyard

and in the wood, that I used to think out loud, or maybe just to myself in silence. I thought about all the things I'd achieved in such a short space of time, and suddenly I didn't know what it was all about, I couldn't attain those final aims I'd decided on. And what did she say? I just remember that smooth cheek. What was she thinking about? Maybe she was seeking something in silence too, and I never had time to ask her what.

'The only thing Caterina will see is the fact that I was unfaithful to her mother. It's only when it involves us that we talk about a crisis, about boredom or lack of understanding; when other people are concerned it's just a banal tale of infidelity. But that's not the point, I want her opinion on the practical consequences of the affair. She'll ask me who the woman was and how I could have done such a thing. But it's the right step to take. I'll go and see her. Maybe for once she'll be able to help me. Maybe she's got experience in these matters. Oh God, how long is it to Christmas?'

In Via Nazionale there were bagpipes playing. But the pipes and pipers were fakes. It was a Christmas job for them.

'Christmas in a fortnight. And what's that boy doing there?'

There was a boy lying on the ground as the crowd passed by. His eyes were glazed and staring. His shoes had holes, his pullover was dirty, as were his hands which clutched a sandwich. He had probably been holding it for some time without eating it.

'Strange, at that age. A fortnight to Christmas. We'll have to invite all the family to dinner. A party with Federica in that state. But at least I'll stay at home for a few days with Marta. This time at least. We'll see about the trip.'

He stopped in front of a building in the city centre.

'Forty-eight. Yes, second floor. How many times have I been here? Three, five at the very most. Ten years they've been married. Ten? I can't remember. Am I doing the right thing?'

He climbed the stairs to the second floor and stopped in front of a door. He looked at the brass name-plate: two surnames, his own and another one.

'Forte. Forte of course. Forte as well but first the other one.'

A twinge of fear kept him from ringing the bell.

'We've never been very close. She's so different, even hostile at times. If I see it's not working, I'll leave at once. What am I afraid of? She's my daughter, after all.'

He put his finger gently to the door-bell. He could hear children's voices within; then light footsteps approaching.

Caterina opened the door, saw her father, and her pleasure and surprise were too intense for her to perceive Forte's nervous, hesitant air.

'Papà,' she said simply, without inviting him in. She gazed at him and almost felt as if she were in the midst of one of those recurring dreams in which she always saw her father just before she woke.

Forte waited for her to say something else. In that

moment he recovered his confidence and detachment.
He entered the flat.

'I'm just dropping in, I don't want to be a nuisance.
I mean if you haven't eaten yet. I must phone home
though, just a quick call.'

Caterina roused herself. 'Yes, we were having
lunch, we've nearly finished . . .' She was embarrassed
and quickly corrected herself. 'Of course you're not
a nuisance.'

'The phone's through there?'

'Yes, I'll show you.'

'No, go back to your meal. I can find it. Just
a sandwich, that's all I need.'

Caterina went back to the dining-room. There were
two boys, almost the same age, sitting there eating
a banana each. Caterina quickly made them get up.

'Through to your bedroom, quickly. Grandpa's
here, he'll come and talk to you later.'

The children mumbled something. Caterina pushed
them gently into their room. There was no time, she
had to hurry, because her father had very little time
and he had come to see her. He had actually looked
her up. She cleared the table, sweeping up bits of bread.
She tried to make it all look neat and ordered.

'He doesn't want much to eat, nothing much. The
salad's finished. What can I get him? A sandwich:
but he didn't really mean that. Maybe he'll be glad
to have something else. But there's nothing ready!'

She was doing nothing right; she put the plates
in the rack and forgot the cutlery; she removed the
half-eaten bread and forgot the napkins. She had a

clear idea of what she would like to do for her father who had dropped in without any warning – like a regular visitor, like her husband. And yet she kept rearranging the knife and fork beside the plate.

'I'm not hungry, don't bother getting anything,' said her father as he came into the room.

They stood there by the table.

'Sit down,' she said. 'There's not very much. We never have much at lunchtime.'

Forte was observing her and discovering little details he had never noticed. First: she was very pretty, dressed for the house, in a brown skirt and pullover, with her hair tied up and her face pale, and no make-up. Second: she looked like him. Everyone said so but he had never seen it. Caterina had her mother's auburn hair and fair complexion. But now he recognised his own eyes, his turned-up nose and his hands. Third: the house was attractive, not too luxurious, furnished in imitation of theirs, but less orderly. He sat at the table, spread out the napkin and took some rice from the plate Caterina held in front of him.

At that moment Caterina was struck by how good-looking her father was. She had never met any man with that same robust, almost rustic air, yet gentle and refined in the way he moved and dressed.

In the expression of his face, Caterina saw a stifled awkwardness which continually contradicted his attitude and his brusque words. If she but thought of it, she felt the tears rise and she couldn't allow this; she had to keep her wits about her, show herself up to the situation.

'I didn't want to bother you,' Forte began, 'because I know how busy you are. I wouldn't have come. But I keep having these strange ideas, strange thoughts. And I wanted to tell you something too.'

Forte let out a deep sigh and looked at his daughter, seeking her help to go on. His courage was failing him. Caterina was following the movements of his lips and hadn't taken in his words: she lowered her eyes and saw her father's hands; they were beautiful, with their gently ageing, transparent skin.

'What's he asked me?' she wondered. 'He can't have said why he's come yet. I must pay attention, my mind's wandering.'

'Federica.' Her father threw the name down. Caterina started. 'It's Federica who's always on my mind. Mamma's told you, I think. She's very worried, she's over-reacting. But *we* mustn't lose our heads, we must think clearly. I don't see things the way she does. I think there's nothing the matter with Federica. She's going through a difficult patch, a complicated one.'

'That's what I think,' Caterina hastily agreed.

'When she was small, you were very close to her, weren't you? You were often together, weren't you?'

'Yes, when she was small.'

'Why? Were things different later?'

'We've seen so little of each other since I got married. Whereas Silvia and I . . .'

'You see,' her father interrupted her, 'I'm very close to her; I've always had great faith in her potential. I've started to think . . . Well, you see, we write each other letters. So even though she doesn't want to talk at

54

the moment, I know — that is, I'm familiar with her thoughts; and you know, there's nothing odd about her. She's very intelligent. She writes to me about her studies. I'm often surprised at the way she thinks. Nothing banal or anything like that, you understand?'

'Yes,' whispered Caterina, and thought that 'anything like that' applied perfectly to herself.

'I don't know many people of her age,' Forte went on, 'but she strikes me as very mature. So the fact that she doesn't want to talk — well, I wonder what it can be due to. I keep asking myself and I get no answer. But I'm convinced it'll pass, it's nothing serious.'

Forte fell silent and stared at the plate in front of him.

'Do you want something else to eat?' Caterina asked.

'Just a spot of cheese. I'm not hungry,' he sighed.

Caterina handed him the cheese-dish and realised it was up to her to say something. After reading the diary she had thought things over, she had talked to a doctor, and now she was convinced that Federica needed help. But the problem now was her father. She didn't want to upset him. She had to speak, but gently and calmly. Whatever else, she didn't want him storming out of the house displeased with her.

'You're right of course,' she said in a low voice. 'I've been thinking about it too. I've spoken to a doctor about it.'

'A doctor?' her father interrupted her in agitation. 'A doctor? What's a doctor got to do with it? Whoever brought doctors into it? What did you do that for? And what did you say to him?' He was furious.

He dropped his fork. It was as he'd always thought, they could none of them look at things calmly. They always had to call in the experts; put themselves into other people's hands and be comforted.

'That's just what the doctor said: there's nothing to worry about.'

'Oh yes? And we had to hear it from him? What did you say to him?'

'I didn't say anything. I just went to him to find out, to try and understand . . .' Her father's hard stare prevented her from going on.

'I'm sorry,' said Forte. 'I'm upset. I came here to let you know something in confidence. But first tell me what the doctor said.'

'He asked a lot of questions about Federica. He told me that he would have to talk to her himself. This kind of dumbness could just be a passing phase. He asked me if she actually found it difficult to speak. I said no. I said she just tried to avoid doing so.'

'She might avoid speaking, but she writes a good deal.'

'Yes. He just gave me some hypotheses based on similar situations.'

'Are there many cases like this?'

'Apparently there have been, over the last few years.'

'They've got their little compartments and they fit people into them. And what else did he say?'

'I didn't understand everything,' Caterina said, feeling embarrassed. 'He talked about behaviour. But anyway he said that if she was able to speak, it couldn't be anything serious.'

'It's a choice she's made.'

'Yes, of course. Then he started talking about me and said I should try and understand why I'd gone to see him.'

'For Federica.'

'Yes, of course. But he claims I have a problem with Federica, from the way I talk about her.'

'And do you?'

'Yes – no. I'm worried, that's all.'

Forte stopped eating. For a moment, gazing into his daughter's eyes, he felt that there was something that needed investigating. But it was too much: one daughter was enough. The thought vanished. Now he had to explain the real reason for his visit. It was getting late.

'When Federica was born, you were seven. Your mother and I weren't getting on too well at the time.'

Caterina started to tremble. Her hands and lips trembled.

'It was nothing serious; it was my fault.' Forte lowered his head. 'I was going through a difficult patch. My work was going badly and I didn't know myself whether I should go on like that or change everything. I was on edge. I wasn't happy with myself and I didn't want any more children. Do you understand?'

Caterina nodded.

'But above all I was confused and I couldn't see things clearly. And Federica was born while I was thinking about other things.'

He paused. He looked at his daughter.

'There was an affair . . . it just lasted a few months.

There was certainly no passion in it. But now it's come back to me and I think, I don't know, I wonder whether it could be . . . Maybe not. They say that you can only tell with these things afterwards. I don't really believe it. But well, I just wanted to talk to you about it.'

He fell silent again. He had got it out.

Caterina was staring at him, her eyes wide. Forte remembered seeing the same expression in that boy's face in the street.

'So do you think this could have been the cause?' he murmured.

'No,' she said at last in a distant voice. 'I don't think so. Don't worry about it. These things happen.'

'I know that. But I meant for Federica.'

'That's what I mean. Did Mamma get to hear about it?'

'Of course. We talked about it at the time, naturally.'

'It's not that then. Don't worry.'

Forte smiled, folded his napkin as if he had finished both eating and talking at the same time. He felt relieved. He suddenly felt very tender towards his daughter. She had helped him and he was grateful to her. He looked at his watch.

'Where are the children?'

'In their room.'

'I must be off. I'll just look in on them.'

Caterina got up. She was happy he was leaving now. Her pent-up emotions were clogging her throat. She wanted this encounter to finish well.

They went into the children's room. The smaller boy was tied to the end of the bed and his brother was pretending – but perhaps not pretending – to thrash him.

'Guido, stop it! You're hurting him!' Caterina shouted, untying the smaller boy. 'Come here, Grandpa's leaving.'

Forte lifted them up one at a time. He kissed them on the cheek. The older one asked him something about his tie; the other boy, shyer and more withdrawn, accepted the hug in silence.

Caterina said goodbye to her father at the door. Forte took her hand. In the darkness of the corridor, Caterina felt she was going to cry.

'Thank you,' Forte said. 'Everything'll be all right, you'll see; Federica will get better.'

He left. Caterina closed the door. She picked up the little boy and kissed him several times and cuddled him.

The bell rang. It was her father again.

'I just wanted to ask you not to tell Silvia about my visit, or your mother. Why are you crying?'

'I'm tired,' murmured Caterina, drying her tears. 'Just tired. Nothing serious. I went to bed late and they woke me early.'

'Go and have a rest. It's my fault for coming.'

'No . . .' said Caterina hoarsely.

Forte closed the door and went quickly down the stairs.

Caterina's husband found his wife with puffy eyes. She was lying on the sofa, smoking cigarettes, one after another. Her husband wasn't expecting this. He'd had a hard day at work. He had talked to his wife on the phone; they had to prepare the Christmas tree, and think about presents.

'I'm worried about Federica,' Caterina said. 'Papà dropped in and we talked about her.'

Her husband went into the bedroom before answering. He took off his suit, tie and shirt. Whatever the calamity – a sick child, money, or a tiff – first he had to strip off his office-armour. He put on a pair of loose trousers and a flannel shirt, choosing a dark one. He already felt depressed. But he was fond of his wife – he loved her and he was ready to dry those tears for her.

He went back into the sitting room, picked up a chair and carried it over to the sofa. 'What does your father say?' he asked gently.

'He's wondering what's behind it all, he's even inventing reasons. He confessed something to me. I didn't want to know anything about it. He's really worried, though he tries not to show it.'

'Let's take things one by one. How's Federica?'

'Please . . .' moaned Caterina. 'Don't let's start all over again, we always say the same things and they're not important. There are other things, so many other things . . .'

'What do you mean?'

'Papà came here without any warning and asked me for advice. No: "I want to tell you something in confidence" was what he actually said.'

'And so?'

'It's strange.'

'What's strange?'

'It's never happened before.'

'What?'

'And now look, look!' she said pointing at the lunch table, the armchairs and the floor. 'The toys, they leave the toys all over the place. Even when I was talking to Papà. Go into the bedroom and see what they're doing! I can't stand any more of it.'

Her husband said nothing. When she was as agitated as that he could never get her to see reason.

'I went to see them. It's even worse than I thought,' Caterina went on, sobbing. 'Federica shuts herself up in her room. Mamma's not well herself and is just waiting for Federica to get better. And Papà comes here and talks to me and then goes off, immediately persuading himself that there's nothing the matter.'

'Can I say something?' he interrupted her. 'It's Federica who's not right, isn't it? Not the rest of you. In fact she says she's fine. But we think there's something the matter. I'll tell you what I think: Federica has been spoilt. She's never been told off. She's never been punished. It's your father's fault. It's all his fault.'

'Why do you say that? You don't know anything about it. You don't know him, you've never talked to him.'

'I know more than you do because I see these things from the outside,' he said, getting heated as if the subject suddenly concerned him closely. 'This business with your sister will be very useful for our children. At least it'll make you realise. Oh, things will be different with them!'

'Why do you say such things? You can't really believe that,' Caterina objected through her tears.

'It's your father's fault,' he repeated categorically, his voice hard. 'It's the way you were brought up.'

Caterina stopped crying. Maybe there was an element of truth in what he said, but her husband's tone of voice betrayed a graver falsehood. She was struck by his total lack of doubt and by an indefinable air of insincerity which filtered through his words. She listened as he spoke. She tried to seize that sensation more firmly. Suddenly she realised that her husband hated her father. Everything he said expressed hatred. He wasn't really talking about Federica's problem, or about his own children, he was trying to demolish her father. The categorical way he stressed certain words was motivated by that sentiment alone.

She thought back to her conversation with her father. And with the doctor. And the discussions with Silvia and her mother. Whenever any of them talked about Federica and her problem, it was their own hidden truths that their words exposed, while Federica was left with her mystery intact.

That evening they talked about their children. Federica was forgotten. Over the next few days, they all met up several times, in groups – every possible combination of their families. Federica no longer stirred from her bed. It was soon clear to the whole family that time and the reassurance of doctors were not helping her to get better. Her mother began to spend long hours staring into space.

Nine

Federica didn't stare into space. Images of her life outside flowed continually across the wall. Previously they had never penetrated her room. Every time she had rung the door-bell or inserted her key in the lock, everything she had done or been through in the previous hours had been erased. She didn't have to make any effort to forget, to avoid being caught out and to maintain her secret. She passed through the doorway and entered upon another life. Just occasionally the smell of her outdoor world would stay clinging to her clothes. Federica would sniff her pullover and coat curiously, and then odd faces, staring eyes and street corners would flicker before her from some remote adventure that had happened to some other person. But then they too would vanish, and the candour of her room, the purity of her thoughts and her books, the perfect immobility of the objects would transform the outside world into an opaque blur of meaningless bustle.

With every step she took towards her room, her desk, her book, her notebook and her bed, her thoughts would settle back into calm regularity. Her mind would resume its ordered neatness.

At school, before university, she had had a group of friends. They used to meet up in her room every day. They used to sit for long hours either in silence or listening to music. Every so often one of them would get up from the bed or the chair, look at the poster for the hundredth time, seeking some new detail; he or she would play with an object in the room, as if attributing some magical powers to it, and then sit down again, smiling at the others and lighting a cigarette. The minutes and hours would go by and then somebody else would go through the same little routine, as if performing some millennial rite.

It had been quite a happy period; occasional moments of unhappiness had occurred within familiar, closed surroundings. In the morning there had been the classroom and her desk. The objects she handled were all childish still: pens, notebooks and texts which were exactly the same for all of them. Sometimes she agreed to let her tongue, her lips and her saliva mingle familiarly with a boy-friend's. On holiday at the seaside she would sometimes find herself sleeping naked next to another naked body, and she would explore the skin and thin legs she already knew from gym-lessons. The sexual organs too, unlike those drawn on walls or shown in magazines, were no different from the lips, hips and armpits; they could be stroked and kissed with detachment.

Feeling perfectly secure and at ease with themselves,

they drifted along in a mental space that stretched to infinity despite having never strayed beyond the perimeter of the house they were born in. In the outside world, as they glimpsed it in chance encounters on trips or along the roads they took daily, they saw contrasts and forms of enslavement that were definitely to be avoided. They suffered most keenly from separations; whoever departed was guilty of a betrayal that brought about their instant dismissal from their hearts.

In appearance they were all such good children; they helped out obligingly and smilingly. They weren't insincere. It never crossed any of their minds that they ought to be bad-tempered or rebellious. They were all united against their elder brothers and sisters with their tales of difficult adolescence. Now everything was familiar and under control.

After school, Federica found herself on her own. She spent the summer by the sea and when she came back to town, she had decided on her course of studies. But there was still time. Over the next few months she still managed to arrange a few meetings with the others. The atmosphere seemed unchanged, and it was better now since they didn't have school timetables.

One October morning she got up early and went off to enrol at the university. In the square in front of the university she studied the graffiti on the walls. There was a cold wind blowing. It flapped posters on the walls and the noticeboards, fluttered the corners of timetables, enrolment-forms and request-notes.

There were several little cards seeking and offering rooms, lessons, motor-scooters. On the driveway people were encamped, selling beads, ear-rings and baubles. Federica stopped here and there to look. She delicately detached a pair of long ear-rings with transparent blue stones from a stall. The boy who owned the stall was lying on the ground.

'Look at yourself,' he whispered, handing her a small mirror with one weary hand.

Federica looked at him. He was very thin; stretched out on the ground, he seemed incredibly tall. He wore red cotton trousers with gold stripes, a Nepalese waistcoat and was smoking a pipe. Federica took the mirror from his hand. His nails were long and grimy with earth.

'You're beautiful,' he said and smiled, displaying yellow teeth.

'Ear-rings make me look common,' Federica replied, touching the other ear-rings on display.

'That's why you're beautiful,' said the boy, sticking the pipe into his mouth and puffing out thick clouds of smoke.

'Do you like common girls?' Federica asked, staring him in the eyes.

'I don't like girls very much,' he said, with a sly smile, his eyes narrowed to slits.

'Do you know where the philosophy faculty is?'

'Straight down the drive and then left,' he answered, stretching out his arm for the mirror and ear-rings.

Federica set off with her hands in her pockets.

At the end of the drive she turned right and came up against a low building. She stopped for a moment to think. She walked round it, looking for the way in. Behind a half-opened door she glimpsed a woman cleaning the floor. She pushed the door gently.

'You'll have to wait for it to dry,' said the woman. 'If it's urgent, you know there's another one by the entrance.' And she pointed back the way she'd come.

'I'm looking for the philosophy faculty.'

'Keep going, it's on the right.'

Federica returned to the main driveway. In the square, near the lake, two students were going over their lecture notes. One of them was reading aloud to the other: 'Inductivistic epistemology is a Lamarckian type of epistemology. It sees learning as a process of instruction, of repetition or practice, by means of which a disposition or belief is formed.'

Federica approached the pair. The student stopped reading.

'Are you looking for something?' the one who was listening asked her politely.

'The philosophy faculty.'

'To the right, by the staircase. But what do you want?'

'To enrol.'

'Then you'll have to go to the administration office. But it's closed now.'

'Closed? It's only ten o'clock.'

'There's a great long queue so they've closed. You'll have to come back tomorrow. Have you got all your papers?'

'Yes.'

'It's easy then. Come early tomorrow morning.'

'Are you doing philosophy?'

They laughed. 'Yes, but we've got way behind in our exams.'

Federica moved off. It wasn't her habit to say thanks; it wasn't rudeness on her part. It was a sign of spontaneity; or at least that was what she thought.

She entered the faculty building to study the course programmes. She had brought a notepad to jot down the set books and timetables. She began systematically from the lower floors. By the time she had reached the third, she felt tired. She sat down to rest on a bench outside the department of theoretical philosophy. There was nobody around. At the beginning of the year – they had told her – there's nothing to do; the lessons begin in November, then there are the Christmas holidays; no exams until June. In the deserted corridor, Federica looked at the walls: the graffiti had been painted over several times, as one could see from the different shades of white; here and there more recent examples stood out. It was difficult to understand them. She went over to the window. From up here one could see the labyrinth of paths and avenues, the lines of stalls, the bustle of students and professors. Where was everybody else? Maybe they were all wandering around asking for information as well. She thought back to afternoons spent in her room, the way she and her friends all understood one another with simple glances.

She felt a sharp and unexpected pain in her chest

as she gazed out of the window; it lasted only a few seconds and then faded into a thought: 'It's natural, you finish school, you go to university. There's nothing strange about it, and besides I can phone them this afternoon, if I want to. I can go on seeing them, and all these people here' – she said to herself, thinking of the passers-by, the boy with the ear-rings, the cleaning woman, the professors whose names were written on the doors of the departments – 'what do they mean to me? Nothing, they don't exist, I'll never meet them.'

A group of women came out of a department, secretaries probably. They were talking about shopping, the last few days of holiday, their sons and daughters on their way back from trips. Federica kept her eyes on them as they went down the stairs, waving goodbye to one another.

A sudden idea startled her: these people of all ages – the two students out there and all the others – all of them were different. They were the kind of people life was made up of, normal people; people she would come into contact with every day. She went running down the stairs. She crossed the square and ran down the drive. She tried to fool herself that once she got out into the street she would see things in the same old way. But she couldn't. She was going to come into contact with all these people. It was a terrible thought. More than anything else she feared their bodies, close now and ineluctable – bodies and smells, all different from hers. They would jostle her, thrust past her, rub up against her.

On the way home, she felt as if she had lost some vital layer of herself. As she strap-hung on the bus, jammed in by the other passengers, she touched her own arm. She rubbed it, and felt nothing.

She went back mentally over all the places she had been to, but it was as if several different Federicas were jostling side by side, never converging. And then, as if she had set off some perverse mechanism, the morning's actions were joined by those of the previous days, and then the days before that, and each time a different Federica appeared. She felt as if it wasn't her own force that kept her upright in the bus, but rather the other bodies, which propped her up and prevented her from drifting free in the closed space.

As soon as she got back to her room, she took her own school-books from the bookcase, fetched her notebooks and photos. She arranged them all on the desk and sniffed the paper. Clutching her white marble egg in one hand, she lay on the bed and waited for her father to return. She didn't know how he could help her. It was ages since they had spent any time together. But Forte had studied at the university and perhaps he still remembered the rules of the institutes, the professors and the various departments. She couldn't ask her sisters to help her: in their days the university had been a political battleground. People had talked about different things then: things that had nothing to do with the university or school, but with a beautifully vague world, comforting in its remoteness and vacuity.

When Forte came back home, the first thing he did was to go along to his daughter's room. Federica had hastily taken her seat at the desk, a book in front of her, as if she had got down to studying right from the very first day.

'So how did it strike you?' he asked with that ironic, magnanimous air he adopted at the office.

Federica turned towards him slowly, and gave him a serious look, without letting anything show. 'I don't know, the first day all seemed a bit confused to me.'

'Don't try too hard to understand. There's no real logic to it all. Get hold of the exam programme and choose the subjects that interest you,' he said, lowering his eyes as he always did whenever Federica gazed hard at him.

That had been the one moment in which she had thought she might be helped. Afterwards she had begun to lie, and with the help of her lies had stood up to a sense of desperation that afflicted her repeatedly, and which was always accompanied by a feeling that the outside world was a meaningless muddle.

She had to work out some way of never really leaving her room, that room which contained her odours, her white marble egg and all those other things as pure and white as the egg. She had to avoid contaminating herself on those occasions when she did leave it, she had to find a way of holding her breath between one plunge and the next, as one did when passing exhaust pipes.

Federica found a system. It wasn't a reasoned act:

in a certain sense it was her father's words that had helped her: 'There's no real logic to it all. Choose a subject yourself.'

The next day she went back to the university. She followed the same route as on the previous day; exactly the same route, because once a road has been picked out by chance, it's more reassuring than the road parallel to it. So she passed in front of the boy selling ear-rings; next on to the fountain where she'd met the two students. There was nobody there now. She stopped and looked at the spot where they had sat. She reached the department of theoretical philosophy on the third floor, where she had happened to sit and rest.

Theoretical philosophy was the first exam. She studied for it without any effort. She immersed herself in the subject as if it were the only exam she had to take. She studied the text-books doggedly and found others in her father's library. At the end of the first year, she could manoeuvre her way through her professor's opinions, those of the authors of the text-books and those of the critics. She followed the course diligently. At the exam she outshone all the other students. As soon as she got home, she put the books back in the bookcase. She realised that as she put each book back into place, it was as if she instantly erased all the concepts she'd just studied.

She followed the same method with the other exams: she studied the subject as if it were a closed system; and since each text furnished her with all the material necessary for its comprehension, it was easy to treat it as if it were the only book left to the human race. It worked well for the first year. The professors were pleased with her: the exclusive way in which she approached their subject was exactly what they wanted. The professors loved her just as her father had done for her originality and intelligence.

She was alone at that time. Studying with other people and talking things over were not the rules of the game at the university. She had to invent another game, one that was utterly different and remote from the previous one. That was what she did.

Ten

————

There were a number of strange people who hung around the university driveways, apart from the students. People selling beads and baubles; groups of drug-addicts lying on the grass or wandering around in search of a fix; clusters of young people belonging to parties and associations; packs of youths who sat smoking on motor-bikes. Groups with indefinable traits in common who transformed the university into a great mixed bazaar.

Federica began to observe them between lectures. One morning she had been accosted by a smiling youth who had asked her for a cigarette. He had hung around for a while to chat. He seemed pleasant, but had then moved off again. Federica saw him join another boy. As they went off together, she had re-called her old group of school-friends, now dispersed.

One spring evening, as she came out from an after-noon course, she saw the boy who had asked her for a cigarette, sitting on top of the low wall opposite the faculty building. He was on his own, smoking, and studying his shoe. He looked as if he were waiting for someone. As she gazed at the solitary figure perched on the wall it was as if she were seeing herself, and she suddenly felt very lonely. She wasn't shy; in fact she had never really understood what shyness was. She had heard of it, but she had never been on such intimate terms with anyone as to be afraid that it could happen with other people.

She went up to the boy with the same simple and friendly air with which she approached everybody.

'Hello, will you give me a cigarette this time?'

'I haven't got one.' He smiled. 'Have I asked you often?'

'Just once.'

The boy held out the one he was smoking. 'Smoke this one.'

His hand was stumpy. The palm looked rough. Federica desired the hand more than the cigarette.

'Come with me,' he said, slipping down from the wall. 'I've got to meet someone. On the way we can buy a pack.'

These were the only remarks they exchanged as strangers. Immediately afterwards, Federica joined up with Marco and shared his activities and rules. Once again, as in her schooldays, a tacit relationship had been established which united them without explanations.

Marco now waited for her every day on the wall opposite the faculty building. He never asked her about the day's lectures nor about her family. Their life together began after lectures, when Federica came down the stairs and saw him there in the distance, sitting on the wall. She would walk towards him slowly, stand there and wait. That brief pause encapsulated her desire that he should be the one to decide when and where they would go now. Barely a minute earlier, Federica had been listening to her professor. Marco knew nothing about that, but in the game that followed he was the one in charge. Federica liked that shift from one master to another.

'Let's go.'

Marco zipped up his leather jacket. Sometimes he took her by the hand and they went straight off; sometimes he would kiss her quickly and suddenly on the lips, without looking at her, childishly but skilfully. His jacket and his mouth held the mixed flavours of the sandwiches he sold at the stall outside the university entrance.

He hadn't been working long at the stall. But all his previous jobs had been in a zone between the university, the hospital and the station: the only area of the city that he knew at all well. The day he had turned up in Rome looking for work he had realised instinctively that the first thing to do was to choose his area. The map of Rome that he'd bought at the station only gave the numbers of the zones, and various other indications that were of no use to Marco. So he had folded it up and put it away in the drawer by the bed in his room at the *pensione* Aurora.

That very first day in Rome, with very little money in his pocket, he had started walking aimlessly down one of the roads by the station. Looking at the shops, occasionally following some passer-by who caught his attention, he had ended up at the hospital. Over the next few days, setting out from there, he had gradually widened the circle of his acquaintances. When he reached the university he had stopped. He particularly liked that place because there were so many people of his own age there, and spending a few hours sitting and smoking on one of the benches in the square gave him the pleasurable feeling that he was one of them.

At the university he ran into Sandro, a law-student still trying to pass the third-year exams. For a few days Marco pretended to be a student himself. Sandro talked unenthusiastically about timetables, courses and exams. Soon he confessed that he hadn't taken any exams for ages and he'd do anything to find a job and get away from home.

So they became friends. Marco got him a job in a shoe-shop where he'd worked for a time. Sandro told his parents he was leaving for France where he wanted to find a job and learn French. Actually he went to live with Marco at the *pensione* Aurora.

The *pensione* was on the second floor of an old palazzo near the station. On the neon sign almost all the bulbs were missing; so instead of PENSIONE AURORA, it read PENS AR. When the S went out as well, the sign became the even more enigmatic PEN AR. These words could often be heard in threatening tones amidst the excited conversations of the Somalians who occupied most of the *pensione*.

Marco and Sandro had become a single person. Marco was taciturn and liked to solve problems rather than talk about them. Sandro, on the other hand, was lazy and talkative. Every evening they talked over the intricate questions that arose from the little extra jobs they did at night to earn a few more lire.

What were these jobs? There were a great many employers. Friends of Marco's, traders, local dealers, strange figures who hung around the *pensione*. There were packages to be delivered, envelopes to be collected, information to be transmitted. But what did the packages and envelopes contain? What were all those items of information and who were they for? Federica never found out.

Sandro and Marco counted the money, shared it out, argued over conditions and people. Federica observed them as they discussed the details; she was sure that they knew exactly what was being exchanged and carried around from one part of the city to another. She wasn't the interfering sort and asked no questions; she trusted them. She liked being kept in the dark. She was their woman.

A week after they had met, Marco took her to the *pensione* and introduced her to Sandro. They went up the stairs arm in arm. Every so often Marco stopped, pushed her up against the wall gently, and entered her mouth as he had done on that first occasion.

Unknown men and women went up and down the stairs; they didn't look at them; some murmured a quick hello to Marco and went straight on past.

Federica let him do as he wanted when they lay on the bed too. Every so often she fondled his neck, and as she did so she felt a strange pity for him.

The only time Marco talked was when they were making love. He held her tight and caressed her, talking the while, as if he wanted to cast over her something of his own that had no name. When they finished he would look her in the eyes.

'We'll have a baby and get married,' he would say, before reverting to his brusque taciturnity.

After that first time together, he gave her a silver-plated anklet, with oriental coloured inlays. He clipped it round her ankle himself, sealing it with a kiss. Federica always wore it, concealed under her trousers.

The silver anklet was the only sign of her life with Marco that entered Guido Forte's house. Federica would touch it every so often, listening as they all talked around her, and she would smile at the conversations of people so remote from her.

How perfect that sign was – inexpressible and perfect. No words of theirs could ever serve to interpret it, to understand it, or to judge it. Only she could understand its meaning. It clearly had one, and it was wonderful not to have to explain it to anyone, to keep it concealed.

One day at the seaside, her mother spotted it. She at once sensed something. Over the years her mother had developed the intuition of a sorceress. When she saw the blackened circle that Federica kept swinging round her ankle, a voice within her spoke out clearly.

'She didn't put it there herself,' and she looked at her wedding-ring. 'A man. But she doesn't have anyone at the moment. Why hasn't she said anything? Hidden under her clothes. A pact. What sort?'

'Who is it?' she would have liked to ask her. But for some time now she had felt uncertain of her own thoughts. She was too embarrassed to say anything.

Afterwards, when Federica fell ill and all their convictions were shattered by the truth, she tried – unsuccessfully – to forget that moment when she had had the solution within reach.

'Is it a new fashion?' she asked her that day at the seaside.

Federica burst into shrill laughter. 'Indian women have worn them for centuries.'

'And why do you wear it?' she asked in that commonsensical way that had already turned her first two daughters against her. But Federica was different from the others.

'If you like, I'll take it off; it doesn't bother me,' she said panderingly, knowing her mother would never ask her to do so.

Her mother questioned Caterina and Silvia about it. She received ironic and reassuring replies.

'Slave-woman anklets. They're being worn now,' said Silvia. 'Hers is in rather bad taste. She probably bought it at the university.'

'There's a fashion for symbols of slavery – symbols which even the women in those countries won't wear. But we see them as mysterious and attractive,'

Caterina said, in that surly tone she had adopted ever since the birth of her second child.

Her mother wasn't interested in how much the anklet cost or in Caterina's sociological theories. Maybe her daughters were more intelligent than she was but they could never see the wood for the trees. However, she pretended to be reassured.

Behind the shadow-line traced by the anklet on Federica's skin, she glimpsed desires that were unknown to her.

She waited for her husband to join them at the weekend and clear up all lingering suspicions.

'It's not her style, don't you agree?' she asked. 'Usually she detests things like that.'

Forte observed his daughter. She was walking slowly towards the sea. Her long, intensely black hair bobbed on her shoulders. His eyes followed her as she dived into the water and swam off confidently.

'It's just her age,' he said.

Her mother closed her eyes in the sun. For just a moment two memories blurred into one another in her mind: Federica's tiny ankle inside its little woollen slipper, when she had bent over her cradle to gaze at her for the first time; and that shrill laugh with which she had answered her question. Then she thought no more about it.

Eleven

Federica was in bed, lying on one side. In the room's half-light, she stared at Caterina sitting in the armchair by the bed. Her sister's eyes were on her but they didn't seem to see her.

Federica's mind, on the other hand, was working feverishly. It scrabbled, trying to remember: Marco, Sandro, the *pensione*, the jobs and then the exams. All those memories had come to an abrupt halt on the day she had taken her philosophy of language exam. That volume by Saussure. Unlike the other exams, she could remember the professor's questions.

'Are you awake?' Caterina interrupted her. She was bending over her. 'Do you want something to eat? Mamma and Papà have gone out to dinner. They'll be back soon.'

For a moment Federica forgot that she was no longer able to decide when to speak and when to keep silent. She tried to answer; but the tongue of glass dropped inexorably inside her throat, driving the air back into her lungs; she felt the wound, the furrow that the tongue had gouged into the walls of her throat. As long as she didn't try to speak, she felt no pain. But if she forgot about it for one instant, and tried to emit a whisper, the tiny calcified lamina at the back of her throat rasped against its walls, reducing her to tears. And for a second or two it was impossible even to swallow.

She showed the doctors the exact spot where it hurt, pointing with her finger. They could see nothing. Her throat was clear and normal. Federica would try to make herself understood, pointing at the spot again. The doctors would bend down to look and still see nothing.

'As soon as she wants to speak,' the last doctor had said, 'she'll be able to. There's nothing the matter.' And lowering his voice he had spoken of 'psychological factors'.

Federica listened as they whispered words like aphasia, neoteny and some others that were even stranger and more complicated.

It was two months since that day she had tried to speak and realised for the first time that she couldn't. Initially she had struggled against it, she had accepted the doctors and swallowed the food she was given. But she felt increasingly certain that her chances of using her voice were dwindling; it had become little more than a hoarse gasp which communicated nothing. So she gave up collaborating.

Caterina gently touched her bare arm where it lay listlessly on the blanket. Federica pulled it away brusquely; she stroked the point where Caterina had touched her as if trying to wipe away the mark.

'If she touches me again, I'll have to hit her. Otherwise she'll go on doing it. I can't stand them touching me.'

'Don't you want anything to eat then?' her sister repeated.

Federica shook her head and closed her eyes.

'She won't be able to say anything to me,' she thought.

She returned to that period when she'd taken the philosophy of language exam. She strove to remember what had happened afterwards. She had tried in vain several times already. Sandro, Marco, the university, home. What had happened after the exam? Her mind refused to move forward. She could recall the previous days and months. And then there was a break. A dark period of unknown length, without any memories.

Sandro and Marco had disappeared. She had asked after them at the *pensione*. The landlord and the people who had known them said they couldn't remember their names. At times Federica thought she must have dreamt them up. She lay on her bed crying. She touched the blackened circle round her ankle: the only sign of Marco that was left her. She wasn't in love with him, just as she hadn't been in love with the others when at school, but she missed his body and it pained her that she had no proof of his existence. What had happened? Why had they gone? What was that threshold beyond which she could only see pitch darkness and shadowy figures running around wildly to escape from a fire? There had been a fire. Federica could see the flames and

84

the people running away. But she knew nothing else, she couldn't remember a single thing.

Her mind refused to go any further, it rebounded from that image without managing to take it in, and it returned to that day when she had taken the exam and then to a later period. Was it much later, or just a short time? When was it that she had taken up her lonely studies again and stopped talking? How much time had passed between those two periods? A day, a month, a year? Before falling ill, she had tried to reconstruct that fragment of empty life by consulting her diary. But there were pages missing from her notebook; it started up again on a certain date which had no special significance for Federica. Her notes, from that date on, talked no more about her life. They were trifling remarks about the university and her family. And the diary, in the pages prior to the gap, said nothing about Marco. Yet Federica remembered writing about him; or at least she thought she did. Who had torn those pages out? Everything went hazy again; the dates and her memories. So she had decided to give up, hoping that she might forget the pages that had been ripped out together with that part of her life with Marco.

Since she'd been ill, all those thoughts had re-emerged: a silent lake in which she swam all alone, seeking handholds, a prisoner of the water that lapped at the shore beyond which her memories disappeared.

'I know you're not asleep because your eyes are moving.'

Her sister's voice made her open her eyes

involuntarily. She closed them again at once, hoping that Caterina hadn't noticed.

'God, please stop her! Now she'll start talking and getting emotional, she'll try to help me just to prove to the others that she's the cleverest. Why don't they come back?'

'When you were little you used to do the same thing, you'd pretend to be asleep but your eyes always flickered.'

Caterina's voice was sweet and far off.

'Do you remember?'

'My God! Make her stop!'

'You used to tell a lot of lies, when you were little,' Caterina went on, talking to herself, as if her sister was not only unable to speak but deaf as well. 'You continued telling them when you grew up, I know.'

'What does she know? Nothing. She's pretending, to scare me.'

'When you were born, I was seven. I used to bath you and change you. I enjoyed it. At the beach I taught you to swim and at night you used to come into my bed. Do you remember? You'd pretend to be asleep but your eyelids flickered.'

Federica stretched out her hand to the bedside table, shifted the glass to the edge and then pushed it over, shattering it. Caterina broke off and looked at the glass on the floor and then at her sister with a dazed air, as if she'd just woken from a dream. She got up to pick up the pieces.

'Did you want a drink?'

'Idiot, cretin, conceited fool.'

'I'll bring you some water.'

She left the room. Federica hid her face under the blankets.

'She doesn't know anything at all. She thinks she can move me with her pathetic line of talk. Let her talk then! I'll plug my ears and that'll be that.'

She pulled open the drawer next to the bed, rummaged in a box and took out some ear-plugs. She stuffed them in just a second before her sister came back. She assumed a seraphic air.

Caterina held the glass out to her. Federica pretended to drink and put it down on the table.

'You don't mind if I talk?'

Federica smiled at her.

'You know, I don't agree with the others when they say there's nothing the matter with you and you're just refusing to talk. Nobody could do that. But I don't want to treat you like an invalid because I don't think you are one. Sorry if I talk to you like this. But over the past few months we've all of us been saying different things. We've all got our own theories, our own opinions, and we just keep pushing them violently as if it was ourselves we were trying to convince. And there's no common ground; we each of us think we know more about it than anybody else, that we understand it better.'

Federica smiled again, as if she'd heard every word. She slipped her hand under the blanket. She caressed her stomach, put a finger to her navel and rotated it like a screw: it was different from other people's, smaller and protruding. Marco used to put his tongue to it, sliding it over the hard point, trying to get inside. Federica felt the warmth of his saliva and saw Marco's head sliding up from her navel to her breasts.

'He couldn't trace me, I'd never told him my surname and he'd never told me his. But he read it once, in my university registration book. He asked me to explain the marks and he laughed at the photo: "You look like a street-girl," he said; and Sandro started laughing too: "Why, isn't she one?" They laughed. But maybe he didn't take it in then, and later forgot all about it. Marco . . .'

Federica closed her eyes and squeezed her breast until it hurt. When she opened her eyes, she saw that Caterina was crying and lighting another cigarette. She shifted one of the plugs slightly.

'. . . so I listened to Papà talking about me, it had never happened before, and he was saying she's clever, isn't she clever, but from the tone it was clear he meant I wasn't worth much. "She's got great maternal sense! She knows how to do that kind of thing, she has no pretensions, but what she does she does well." '

Caterina paused, looked at her sister, and moved closer to the bed. Federica slid down under the blankets.

'Am I tiring you, talking like this? Do you want to sleep?' she asked, sitting on the bed.

Federica didn't move.

'Do you want me to go on talking?'

Federica nodded. Caterina settled herself at the foot of the bed, resting against a heap of pillows.

'Before that it had never crossed my mind that you had to behave in a certain way if you wanted his favour. His study bored me. I didn't like the games he kept in the wardrobe.'

'Memory-stirrer. That's all she can do. We've got absolutely nothing in common.'

She plugged her ear, pushing hard on the wax so that her sister's voice was blotted out completely.

'He couldn't find me. Of course not. But why did he disappear? Where did they both go?'

Federica's mind refused to go any further. In fitful gleams, illuminated by a light that had nothing to do with logic, she saw that incomprehensible scene: people running from a fire. It was like a scene from a film, in the way it seemed both remote from her and immediate, as if she had been present. Something had happened the day of her philosophy of language exam; or maybe not the very same day. But when? She couldn't go on. Her mind skipped over that period, and it found no further memories until months later, when she had returned to her studies and had then slipped into this empty silence.

Up to the day of the exam she could follow her life clearly: her life with Marco and Sandro; and that separate life with the others who knew nothing.

Marco had become taciturn and brusque. He treated her badly. His mood changed as if there were some permanent worry on his mind that wouldn't allow him to relax or be gentle. Sandro was beginning to get frightened of him too. What did Marco do all day long? He had left his job at the bar. He no longer needed it, so he had told her. He earned enough with his other jobs around the neighbourhood.

Federica at last asked him what they were. They were lying on the bed at the *pensione*. Marco looked at the row of battered windows and the aerials on the building opposite. Federica had the feeling that his words were loaded with a special gravity and that his eyes were seeking a way of escape.

'Things are getting tougher,' he had replied.

She would have liked to ask him about those jobs again, what they were and who commissioned him, but she was afraid of being treated badly. And anyway it was wrong to muscle into someone else's life with questions. Everybody has his or her good reasons. One mustn't pass judgement or ask questions.

She just asked him if he needed money. Marco pulled a wad of fifty-thousand-lire notes from his pocket.

'I can buy you something if you want,' he said.

Marco met Federica after work. He had never involved her in his business. Sometimes, when some unexpected job cropped up, he would get Sandro to wait for her on the wall outside the faculty building.

Every time she saw him in the distance, perched on top of the wall, as on that first occasion, she tried to guess his mood. The first time she saw Sandro in his place, she realised she was glad. Sandro was waiting for her in front of the entrance. He was dreamily contemplating rather than reading the noticeboards, as if the layout of the lecture timetables recalled to him his own past as a student.

'You interested?' Federica asked him.

'No, I was just looking,' he answered, going red. 'Marco was busy, we can join him later at the bar.'

They sat on a bench to smoke. Sandro asked her about the course, and got her to show him her notes and the textbooks. He passed his hand over the closely-written pages.

'When I studied I used a highlighter. That way I only read the important bits.'

'I don't like highlighters. I use the same pen I had at school, only they don't make them any longer,' sighed Federica, imitating her father's tone when he talked about new products that didn't come up to the standards of old ones.

'My father's a teacher and my mother keeps a stationery shop. If I could only go back there, I could get you as many pens as you want.'

'When did you last see them?'

'A year ago. I didn't like studying. It's a question of brains, perhaps. I just couldn't make any headway. My father – you know, a teacher – he couldn't understand it. Marco helped me get the job. They're convinced I'm in France. A friend of Marco's works in France and he sends them a telegram every so often. I mean, they know I don't like writing letters.'

With his head bowed, Sandro continued to gaze at Federica's notebook.

'How many exams have you taken?' he asked her in a small voice.

'Two. I'm preparing for three more at the moment.'

'It's as though they never finish,' he sighed. 'You take one and you've got fifteen more ahead of you. To tell you the truth, I only ever took three in all. So I don't really know what it feels like to have taken any more. The only exam I liked was the history of Roman law. Maybe because it was the first. It started off on definite lines and you just kept following it through – it was clear-cut. With the other exams I could never understand whether it was a question of what the book said or the Civil Code, and which way you had to put it to the professor. I always got it wrong at the exam. It's all a matter of brains. I just get confused.'

'No, it's not that at all,' said Federica, putting her books away. 'You have to read the first few pages quickly and then go into them a bit deeper. In the lectures you have to find out what the professor thinks and then underline it in the book, so that in the exam you know what he wants and just repeat it. It usually works.'

They got up and set off to meet Marco.

From the very first day they decided tacitly that there was no point in telling him about their conversations. A secret terrain was at once created between them, which consisted, as far as they were concerned, of a common nostalgia for notebooks and lessons, schoolroom chit-chat, far beneath Marco's manly maturity. They were children compared with him.

Sandro took up his studies again without even realising it. At first he asked Federica questions with the book in hand. He realised that he was able to grasp the concepts quickly and remember them. He gradually became enthralled by the course, like a thriller-reader approaching the denouement. He was enthralled by Federica too, by her matter-of-fact way of talking, by the way she bit her fingernails, twisted her black hair into a great knot at the back of her neck and held it there with a pencil. He realised he had been totally enthralled that day when Marco had kissed Federica on the mouth in front of him, something that had never happened before. Their friendship didn't allow for shows of affection. But on that occasion Marco's eyes had been bright as if with fever.

So for the first time he felt both jealous about Federica and sorry for his friend.

'Marco's not well,' he said to Federica one day, sitting down next to her on a bench.

They talked about Marco's jobs. Sandro didn't know much about them either.

'It's Pino who gives him the jobs and the parcels; he deals in household appliances. We went along together once. He lends him his scooter too. He's promised to give it to him. He's got loads of money and he's crazy about scooters.'

'What are these parcels?' Federica asked, her natural reserve failing her for once. 'Are they spare parts?'

'No, because they don't weigh anything. It's Pino's private business. He's got a hand in all sorts of things. His shop has got two doors: one for people buying household goods and the other one that Marco uses for his parcels. There are always lots of people. It's a kind of agency. A lot of Africans too.'

'And the parcels?' she asked again.

'He has to take the parcels to the forwarding office at the station, see to everything and then bring back the receipts. But Marco does a lot of other jobs for him.'

'But what's inside the parcels?' Federica insisted.

'I don't know. Maybe just paper, because they don't weigh anything. And anyway there's another office at the station for heavy things.'

They fell silent for a while, both still wondering what those weightless parcels could contain. Then they started talking about exams again.

'You could enrol next year. I'll do all the paper-work for you. In the meantime you could prepare for an exam.'

'No, I've chucked it in. And anyway, what would be the point?'

'It would be a help to me, so I wouldn't be studying on my own. Really, we could study a bit here and at home I'd do a summary for you.'

Sandro was looking at her. As she talked Federica had removed the pencil from her hair so that it swung free over her shoulders. Now she was using the pencil to doodle in her notebook – a house, a tree, some flowers – like a child. She looked up at Sandro and stared at him emotionlessly with her glinting black eyes.

Sandro's eyes dropped and he saw her hand drawing absently on the paper. Trembling inwardly, he touched it. His hand was smaller and thus it ended up nestling inside hers. Sandro pressed his thin lips to Federica's. They were soft and slightly parted, on account of her protruding lower lip, which gave her a perman-ently sulky look. They walked along the university avenues.

Sandro took her to his parents' stationery shop in

Trastevere. He watched her from a distance, hiding round the corner.

'Was my father there?' he asked her afterwards, in a state of some excitement.

'Yes, he was.'

'Who served you?'

'Your mother. She looks like you.'

'Well, they're my parents all, after all.' And he laughed to hide the effect of those words on him: 'She looks like you.'

As they walked along he got her to describe them to him in every way possible.

Such moments between them never lasted long. Both of them soon felt the urge to go and see Marco.

The moment they saw him at the station bar, chatting to the barmen while he waited, they would feel a twinge of guilt – not for the kisses but for those shared memories, things that Marco would never understand, for Sandro's notebooks which Federica now kept in her bag together with her own.

They knew nothing of Marco's memories. He had never told his story to anyone.

So the months went by for her: mornings at the university, afternoons with them, and evenings at home.

As the exams approached, Federica occasionally saw them in the evening instead of the afternoon, always between the bar and the restaurant at the station. Sometimes they went to the cinema. They formed a trio.

Sandro had become a working student and now he was almost sorry that his parents believed him to be in France.

'Philosophy of language.' Federica rummaged through her memory. 'That book of Saussure's, we studied it together. And then? What happened then?'

Everything turned hazy again; and if she tried to push forward by sheer willpower, she found her previous memories fading as well, those that had been clear up to a moment ago; it was as if, whenever she attempted to cross the threshold of the last illuminated room, someone amused himself by turning off the lights behind her too.

Federica squeezed her breast with one hand. As soon as she felt the warmth of her skin, her memories of Marco returned. The tip of her toes bumped against her sister's body. She looked at her: Caterina was talking; her lips were moving swiftly. Every so often they would pause, grip the end of the cigarette tightly, and dilate at the corners in a grimace of pain.

'Like the television with the sound turned down. Now we're in the same situation, she's talking and I can't hear her. I'm thinking and I can't talk. But it doesn't make any difference. It was exactly the same beforehand.'

For a second there flashed across her mind the image of that game she used to play with her sister: Caterina used to lie there and lift her up with her feet and then suddenly let her come crashing down on top of her. Now Federica wouldn't want to touch her with the tip of her finger. She was repelled by the way she talked, the way she was perpetually on the verge of tears – just like her mother. At least her mother didn't talk so much. She decided that Marco was the only person she would ever allow to touch her. After all, he was bound to turn up again some time. An address can always be tracked down, if one really wants to. And if he didn't come back – well, nobody else.

Once again she saw herself lying on the bed in the *pensione*, the day he had found out about her studies with Sandro and their walks together.

'Sandro told me he wants to take an exam with you,' he had murmured to her, his eyes gazing out of the window.

He was holding her tight; Federica's face was nestling between his shoulder and his armpit.

'Just to keep me company. He's got nothing to do in the afternoon. He didn't really want to. I told him he should.'

Federica lifted her face to the hollow in Marco's neck, and looked up at him.

'Are you fonder of him than me, now that you're studying together?'

Federica stroked his neck; she closed her eyes and breathed in the odour of his skin. 'If you want, I'll chuck in my studies, it doesn't bother me.'

'Your parents,' said Marco – and it was the first time he'd ever mentioned them, 'do they know you come here?'

'No. But we never talk about these things. They don't think I've got that many friends.'

'We could look for a flat. Me, you and Sandro, now I've got the money. I've got loads more.'

'Those parcels you take to the forwarding office

at the station – do you know what's in them?' Federica asked, gazing out of the window like Marco.

He didn't reply; he remained motionless for a few seconds and then abruptly turned on one side.

'No, I don't know,' he said harshly. 'Are you unhappy about my work? Do you want me to start studying too?' He laughed. 'There are thousands of students, why don't you screw one of them? Are they no good at it? They spend too much time studying. Before you came along I knew another girl who studied, she used to come here in the afternoon, just like you. In this room.'

He turned towards her to see the effect this was having.

'You never told me,' said Federica, showing no emotion.

Her eyes gazed at him; they were questioning and calm.

'Why do you come here? Just to make love? I love you, why don't you . . .' Marco said, his voice cracking as he pulled her towards him, 'don't you love me?'

He held her so tightly she felt her spine might break. Federica tried to nod by way of answer, but all she managed was an incomprehensible toss of her head.

'Why do you never say so?' he said again.

Federica's eyes were still calm and cold but glazed with tears. 'I don't know,' she whispered without even moving her lips. She wished fervently that he would hug her, hold her tight again and stop staring and talking. She wanted to go back home to her room. She squeezed her hand into a fist as she did when clutching the white marble egg.

'I don't know,' she repeated, starting to cry silently and to tremble.

Marco slid on top of her. Federica thought of her father and the advice he always gave her: 'Don't alienate yourself from yourself,' he used to say. 'Never sacrifice your own critical capacity, your own mind, to anyone; keep it free, don't let it submit to anything.'

Marco's head slid round her taut neck, over the fine skin between her breasts, her navel, between her legs.

'Don't alienate yourself from yourself, alienate yourself from yourself, yourself . . .' She lingered over the words like a song-refrain.

She closed her eyes. For a second she felt it was her father kissing her in this fashion, and she was instantly ashamed of the thought and squeezed her eyes tighter. She imagined her father's face at such an idea. But anyway, who could ever tell him, it was only a thought. And who could ever tell Marco that she was thinking such things at that moment? Or Sandro. Or her mother and anybody; no one. No thought.

'Marco's bound to come looking for me,' thought Federica in her bed. 'And we'll go on that journey together.'

There rose up before her mind that unspoilt vision she preserved deep within herself like a postcard: the barefoot women walking over the red earth with their children hanging round their necks. Coloured cotton cloths round their thin bodies. That sense of simple tranquillity, of a harmonious relationship with the world of objects, as laid down by established laws. 'Thou dost preserve the stars from wrong; And the most ancient heavens, through Thee, are fresh and strong.' She remembered the poem she had found in her book of Indian philosophy.

'Yes, I'll get better there.' She stretched her legs out to the end of the bed. She no longer felt her sister's body. She opened her eyes. Caterina was standing by the window, staring out in silence.

'Maybe she realised I wasn't listening.'

She took her plugs out quietly. Caterina said nothing for a few more seconds, and then, as if she had been collecting her thoughts, continued a sentence she had broken off halfway.

'. . . yes, in fact everything he disapproved of, I disapproved of too. It's made me hard and unhappy. To have given my life away in such a hurry, and ended up feeling stupidly resentful against everyone. It all stems from him. All of us obliged to desire highly intelligent things. If you don't make the grade, you're condemned to mediocrity. Out of the game, in his eyes. Of course you go wrong, you're bound to, you end up deliberately looking for mediocrity. You try to show it's been a matter of choice, let him see you can do something different but just as intelligent. But it's no use because it's not true. Anything you do just to make a point is always wrong. Right and wrong at the same time. Wrong for the person who does it, right as a matter of principle. But principles are never of the slightest use to anyone.'

Caterina took out another cigarette. She realised that Federica was looking at her. She started talking again at once, inhaling the smoke deeply; her eyes were dilated and her voice became more and more agitated, insisting nervously on certain words.

'So what part of our lives is it that gets left out, that isn't considered intelligent? Those of us who have had children know the answer to that. Yet I've never managed to prove it to him. He never listens to anyone, he doesn't give you anything of himself, he doesn't talk, he doesn't mingle. He has his ideas and he never reveals them to anyone. Sometimes I've even thought perhaps they don't exist. You always have to prove to him that you've understood, that you haven't missed a word, that you're ready for anything. Detachment. That's his password. Can you be intelligent if you're emotional, if you get involved in things, or if you cry easily?'

Caterina looked at her sister, her eyes misty with tears, her cigarette trembling in her fingers.

' "What you've done is irrational." That's what he says. And he means weak, sentimental: everything is weak and sentimental in the end. But it doesn't matter, none of this is important any longer. Despite everything, I still want his attention and I've done everything not to get it. I've not been intelligent enough. And you have to be very intelligent to make him love you and to become as strong as he is. So you see, in the end, he's the one who's right all along. Now I can't be good any longer. It's terrible, to be incapable of goodness.'

'That's the way I am too,' thought Federica involuntarily.

'You can't be good if you're as weak and senti-mental as I am. You long for the worst for yourself and for other people, you long for some disaster to make you feel better. Like Mamma who can't talk now without crying.'

Caterina wiped her tears away with her hand and put out her cigarette in the ash-tray. She bent down so that her face was close to her sister's.

'Do you think something like this has happened to you?'

Federica stared into her eyes. Caterina took her hand.

'Don't you think it's something like this?'

Federica shook her head, but inadvertently left her hand in her sister's.

'When you started to feel ill, it may seem strange, but that's when I started to feel better. I realised that for the first time he was affected by it and we could all talk about something painful. So I got better.'

'Pain-stirrer,' thought Federica hatefully.

She put a hand to her throat. The walls of her throat seemed to be squeezing together and sticking to one another. She started to cough and thrash about, floundering for air. Caterina tried to sit her up. Federica writhed and kicked off the blanket, clutching at her throat. A dry cough shook her whole body. Caterina tried to pull her up again. But her sister's body was rigid. She took fright and started to call her name. She suddenly fell silent and turned round; her father and mother were at the door.

'What's the matter?' said Forte, moving to the bed.

Her mother remained in the doorway.

'Just now, she suddenly got taken like this and started coughing.'

'How do you expect her to breathe with all this smoke?'

Forte threw the window open. He returned to his daughter and forced her to sit up. Federica started breathing.

'Couldn't you do without a cigarette for a few minutes?'

'But I've hardly smoked at all . . .' Caterina protested.

'The ash-tray's full. It's bad for you too.'

Forte laid his daughter down again and pulled the blanket up around her. Her mother rearranged the bedclothes. Caterina stood and looked at her sister for a moment from the door: now she seemed calmer. She left the room.

She went and sat in the living-room. From a table next to the sofa she picked up a small silver tree; every branch held a swinging oval frame, five photographs in all. She put it on the table and watched as their five smiling faces swayed to and fro and then gradually settled back into quiet symmetry. She lit a cigarette.

Twelve

'Have they explained what neoteny means? Have they told us clearly?'

Forte lit a cigarette. He looked at all the members of his family, one by one, sitting on the living-room sofas.

'They've told us, Guido,' said his wife, her voice hoarse from lack of sleep.

Observing her two daughters and their husbands, Signora Forte felt serenely satisfied. They had all come. It was so rare for them all to be together. If only Federica were there too, instead of shut up in her room without saying a word. But then if Federica weren't ill the others wouldn't have come.

'Neoteny, literally: the retention of infantile features, one of which is aphasia,' said Silvia, repeating phrases she had read in the medical encyclopaedias.

'And so? Literally! What are we supposed to do?' yelled Forte, staring at his daughter with furious eyes. 'How many doctors have you consulted? Have we made any progress?'

'Guido, don't get angry! Silvia's trying to understand things, like the rest of us,' put in their mother.

'No, go on. Let him go on, Mamma,' said Silvia in a hard voice. 'Go on, what do you think then? That the doctors are wrong? There's nothing the matter with Federica?'

'They use vague words. They don't give us any remedies, they don't tell us anything. So it's better not to take any notice of them.'

Caterina and Silvia both lit cigarettes.

'Maybe we should have followed just one of them,' said Silvia's husband in an attempt to calm his wife.

'Don't smoke like that!' said Forte, putting out his cigarette and getting up to open the window. He paced up and down in front of the open window. They all looked at him, aware that he was looking for someone to get angry with.

Caterina's husband expressed his opinion. 'I think the best idea is just to leave her alone, not let her see that she is the centre of our attention. We should have followed what Murialdi said. He's got a lot of experience. He's sure that Federica's deliberately chosen not to talk. He's convinced that Federica, like a lot of other girls of her age, hasn't been brought up with enough . . .'

He was searching for the least offensive words. Forte had halted by his side and was gazing at him.

'Well?' he said, trying to keep his voice calm.

'Well, Federica's always been completely free! There's never been adequate control over her and she's never had any constraints. And lots of others like her!' He was roused by the expression of contempt he could see on Forte's face. 'And that's what Murialdi said.

But I think so too, I've always thought so. You have to teach children to keep quiet at times if you want them to know how to talk as adults.'

Unwittingly he had found the right phrase, a highly appropriate image for the situation.

Forte continued to gaze at him and say nothing; everyone was watching him, waiting to hear how he would answer.

'So, as you put it, we should teach children to keep quiet, we should keep them in their place. Very nicely put,' said Forte, almost to himself, as if he really were reflecting on his son-in-law's words. 'And we should also pretend not to be worried. Just as we should have been stricter when she was small. More authoritarian, even if we weren't really sure whether it was right or not. And now we ought to hide our pain in seeing her like this. It's strange that *you* should be telling *me* this. You're thirty-five and I'm sixty. Falsehood as a principle for bringing up children. I've never believed it!' He was shouting now. 'Listen to me, all of you. You two as well!' he said, addressing his daughters. 'I clearly haven't managed to make you see anything. I can only teach what I am, nothing else. I've tried to teach you that you must use your own heads. Do you want a code of behaviour that's certain, that can't be questioned? That's all lies. That's what we had and we grew up like terrified little brats. Ten years of my life were wasted in shaking off fear and you want me to teach that to my daughter! Nobody will ever make me believe that's right.'

He sat down, exhausted. His wife looked at her

two daughters. Unseen by her husband she signalled to them to say nothing, not to insist. There was a long silence. Those who weren't smoking lit up. Forte took a cigarette himself. His hands were visibly trembling. Silvia's husband, sitting next to him, lit it for him. He couldn't hold it still in the flame.

'But perhaps she isn't really ill. Why should she be? Why didn't it happen to you two?' their mother murmured.

Silvia took her hand. Once again they all held their tongues. Nobody knew what to say. They all felt the inadequacy of their pet theories and mentally contradicted the ideas they would have liked to express. So they held their tongues.

Silvia caressed her mother's hand. She had aged so, she was so defenceless. She felt suddenly resentful towards her sick sister. Maybe Federica's illness was due to something that didn't involve them at all, something alien to them. She was ill because she was different from them.

'She's got no right to upset our lives like this,' she thought.

'The family can't be held responsible for everything,' she said.

'I've been thinking the exact opposite over the last few days,' her husband murmured timidly.

'How do you mean?' Silvia asked at once.

'I don't know. Maybe it's nothing, but I think that even before Federica fell ill, she was silent.'

He said no more but looked at them all as if he was afraid he'd said something banal.

'And so?' Caterina said at once with a scornful air.

Forte pondered over his son-in-law's words. 'None of us thinks she fell ill just like that,' he said. 'There must have been a time when we didn't notice anything.'

'Maybe she had thoughts that she couldn't tell you,' Silvia's husband concluded.

'So it could be something she wants to keep hidden?' their mother asked.

'I don't know, Marta,' said Silvia's husband gently.

'I've had enough of this!' Caterina's husband burst out heatedly. 'All this wondering over things that don't exist! Things that won't get us anywhere. Just because we don't want to face up to a few simple truths and admit that mistakes have been made. The complete lack of any authority! Continual tolerance! And here we are talking over our feelings and our stupidity!'

'That's enough!' shouted Forte, rising to his feet. 'Get out! Out of my house!'

They all rose together and there was a confused meshing of voices. Caterina's husband had fallen into a stunned silence.

'Guido! What are you saying? Calm down!' Signora Forte came up to the two of them, trying to cool things down.

'I'm going, don't worry. I'll be glad to go, very glad!'

Caterina's husband walked out of the room, forgetting that his wife was still there.

'Papà! Do something! Call him back!' pleaded Caterina to her father.

Forte looked at his daughter and wife. He sat down without saying anything.

Caterina's husband reappeared at the door. He had put his coat on. He looked at his wife and nobody else.

'Caterina, let's go. It's getting late.'

'We're leaving too,' said Silvia. 'It really is late.'

'No, wait, please. Nothing's been decided. Don't go,' pleaded their mother.

'Yes, nothing's been decided. But we must go, it's late.'

They went up to their mother one at a time to kiss her. Forte was sitting on the sofa staring at the floor. He looked old and tired.

''Bye, Papà,' Silvia said without approaching him.

A moment later they were all four in the street. They said goodbye to one another but nothing else, and bustled into their cars.

Silvia saw her sister's car pass them and heard Caterina crying and inveighing against her husband.

She watched her husband start the car, unhurriedly, meticulously.

'You do it on purpose, don't you?' she said. 'You want me to be the one who says all the unpleasant things. You want them to think I've got no feelings. Is that what you want?'

'What do you mean, Silvia?'

'You want Papà to hate me! You want to be the nice one, don't you?'

'You're crazy, Silvia? What are you saying?'

Silvia stared up at the illuminated windows of the house, and kept her eyes on them until the car turned the corner.

Thirteen

_____

Forte and his wife were left in silence, not looking at each other. Forte sat in the same position as when his daughters had left, with his hands raised to his forehead. His wife stared at a non-existent point on the wall, in the gaps between the squares. She would spend hours like that, pursuing vague thoughts which intertwined with one another, knitted together and then unravelled like fraying strands of cloud. She never did it when her husband was around. When he was there she tried to show herself as alert and busy.

Suddenly she realised she wasn't alone. She looked at him. Nobody had helped him, he was alone. But she didn't feel any compassion towards him. She felt compassion for herself, for her daughters who had left, for the youngest one asleep in her room. Not for him. She felt him to be alien and guilty. Generally it was different: she knew that he wasn't perfect, that he posed and pretended, but none the less she usually felt compassion towards him and loved him. She followed the line of wrinkles on his forehead. 'There's no generosity in his pain,' she thought.

'He's humiliated them, them and me, and now he's suffering himself. It's my fault. Ever since I stopped telling him things. How long is it since I talked to him?'

'Guido, I'd like to talk to you,' she heard herself say.

Forte slowly raised his eyes towards her.

'I'm very cross with you,' she started off, picking her words slowly. 'Yes, I think you were wrong to talk to him like that. You shut him up, you made him leave the house. What right did you have to make him go like that? You invited them all here and then drove them all out. Why won't you listen to them? Will you ever listen to anyone but yourself?' she suddenly asked, her voice shrill. 'You don't love them, Guido. They're – we're all unimportant to you. Otherwise how could you have let them go like that? How could you watch them leave without saying a word?'

'Marta,' he broke in. 'We can't let this business with Federica drive us all mad.'

'That's the way it is, Guido. I know. I know that you're not well either. Today, before they came, I told them so. They've got their own children, they can't feel this problem as closely as we do. It's different for them. But what they say . . .'

'What did you tell them?' he interrupted her again.

'To be nice to you, not to be too hard.'

'What did you do that for?' Forte broke in. 'Let them say what they think! Let them talk! Do you think I'm afraid of them? Can't you see that they all came here knowing exactly what they were going to say? That's all they care about. Can't you understand that?'

'No, it's not like that. You're the one who doesn't understand. Caterina told me you went round to see her.'

'And so?' he said, blushing.

'Well, nothing. She was glad you called.'

'She didn't tell her anything,' he thought. 'Maybe I've been too hard on them this evening.'

'Guido, they're just waiting for you to talk to them.'

'What's that? Are you saying I've never talked to them? I've always treated them . . . I've tried to . . . Look, that's the last thing you can say!'

Forte's mind couldn't find the right words. They had discussed this on other occasions. On one point at least he had been clear. Marta had always wanted to keep the girls by her side at all costs. She resorted to all sorts of strategies to ensure they remained like small girls seeking affection and needing her. Once it had been settled that this was the nature of their relationship, she was capable of great understanding and sympathy.

'Let them sort it out by themselves,' he would say to her in bed, whenever she talked to him about some problem the girls had.

'That's what it is,' thought Forte. 'That was why his wife was reproaching him. Because he wasn't like her: condescending, sympathetic. That was what she meant when she said, "They're just waiting for you to talk to them." Once he had got his wife's position clear in his mind, his own was clear too.'

'Why do you get so concerned about them?' he said.

'You worry whether they're offended, whether I've hurt them; you tell them to be good to me, you tell me to be good to them, and you end up by finding fault with everybody. Why don't you think a bit about what we say to each other? About what you yourself think? Whether you feel something is right or wrong? This way you're always setting yourself above us all.'

'I don't think anything's right or wrong any longer,' his wife murmured.

This stung Forte like a whiplash. So that was how she felt too. She who had always been so sure of herself, who had always acted so instinctively, without thinking too much. She felt that way too.

'Sometimes I don't listen properly to what you're saying to each other,' his wife went on. 'But I know it all anyway. Caterina's always looking for something to say to contradict you. If she can just manage to provoke you, she feels better. Silvia takes my side to divide us.' With these last words, her eyes filled with tears. 'As the years go by that's all I can see in your arguments. They want you and you're afraid to get any closer to them.'

'So, in your opinion it's all a matter of "feel-ings",' said Forte, separating the syllables as if he were dictating. 'And nobody in this house thinks anything! Nobody talks! There's never any exchange of opinions! Just a question of feel-ings. I believe the exact opposite: they're weak and angry because they haven't grown up, despite their children, their husbands and their jobs!' He was shouting again. 'And I reckon you're happy when things go wrong for them, when they come crying to you, you're happy to see me in this state now! You've always wanted them to make mistakes so that you could be the first to understand them. You've spent your whole life doing this! And now you're glad Federica's ill.'

He suddenly stopped. His wife closed her eyes, trembling. Forte touched her hand.

'Marta, forgive me,' he whispered.

His wife moved her hand away from his. She opened her eyes: they were cold.

'This whole business, Marta, it's making us say things we don't believe. We're going mad, forgive me.'

'It's the truth, Guido, you spoke . . .'

'No, forgive me, I'm not thinking straight, I'm overstating things.'

His wife looked at him for another second. 'I'm tired now.' She got up. 'I'm going to bed.'

She walked to her room. From the living-room Forte heard the key turning in the lock.

'Just like all those years ago,' he thought. He felt relieved that she wasn't waiting for him in the bedroom.

He started pacing the living-room, his mind drained. He gazed at the books, the pictures and the photographs like a guest awaiting his host.

He stopped in front of a leather-framed photograph of Federica. It was a recent one. She was smiling; one hand was raised to her forehead, pushing away a loose strand of hair.

'One of her gestures,' he thought.

The dark, half-closed eyes smiled sadly as if they were aware of something unknown to the rest of the face.

'The only thing to do now,' he thought, '– the only important thing – is to get her back to what she was.'

He left the living-room, hurried down the corridor and slowly turned the handle of Federica's door.

There was a small light on. The bedside table held eau-de-Cologne, talcum-powder, medicine and alcohol. The room was impregnated with their smells. Forte felt as if he were entering the room of his newborn daughter.

He approached the bed. She was lying on one side, her head towards the wall; her hair hung down, revealing her neck; her arm rested along her side. Her hand was closed tight; Forte saw the white marble egg. Her arm had become so thin that the skin lay in creases and showed the line of the bone. He leaned over to see her face and in doing so jostled the bed. Federica turned towards him, startled. When she saw him she smiled, her eyes opening wide, filling her face. She pulled herself up with an effort.

'Were you asleep?' he asked her.

Federica shook her head.

'Shall I leave you to sleep?'

Federica made a negative gesture. Forte sat on the edge of the bed.

'They all came round this evening. Did you hear us?'

Federica didn't answer; her face darkened.

Forte looked at the phials on the table, the desk with its open books and the panel of photographs. 'Maybe you should take up your studies again,' he said. 'It would do you good. The doctor said you can go out and you ought to. It can't be doing you any good to stay shut up in here all day. Don't you want to go out? Would you like to go out with me some time?'

Federica lowered her eyes to her hand and started to play with the marble egg.

'What's that? Show me.'

Federica handed it to him.

'A marble egg for darning socks,' he smiled. 'Do you darn socks? Then you're the only woman who still does.'

Federica returned the smile.

'Mamma gave it to you, years ago, didn't she?'

Federica nodded and took the egg back from his hands.

'So you don't want to go out? Just stay in bed. What about going away somewhere? Would you like to go away?'

Federica's face lit up.

'So you really would like to go somewhere. Where? I could take a few days' holiday. Would you like to go to the house on Ischia? It'll be cold perhaps, but we could light the fire; I can phone and get them to prepare the house.'

Federica suddenly grabbed his hand. Forte broke off. His daughter's eyes were staring at him lucidly. Federica slid between his arms and laid her head on his shoulder. Forte felt an inner tremor. He pulled her towards himself clumsily.

'We'll go then,' he murmured into her ear. 'We'll go straightaway, without waiting for anything.'

Part 2

Fourteen

S ilvia's husband opened the boot and started to take the suitcases out. Forte glanced at Federica asleep in the back seat. He got out of the car. The quay of Mergellina was deserted, very different from the way he knew it in summer, when he had to push his way through perspiring crowds to catch the last hydrofoil on a Saturday night. He walked slowly along the jetty towards the ticket-office. He stopped when he reached the first row of boats; there were sailing-dinghies, motor-boats and a few larger yachts. Their fenders knocked against the posts and pressed against the coloured buoys, which quivered in turn like a column of chained men.

'What on earth do they do with such big boats?' wondered Forte, examining the equipment, the folded sails, and the control-panels, with their plethora of knobs and switches. 'Just for a quick swim out at sea. A rowing-boat would do just as well.'

He looked up at the Panamanian flags fluttering from the pennants. He smiled as he always did when he came across another confirmation of Italian malpractice.

In these cases — he had confessed it to himself on occasions — what he really felt was satisfaction in having rumbled the dishonest rather than indignation at their dishonesty.

On the jetty two young boys were squatting on the ground, selling cigarettes and lottery tickets. They eyed Forte, wondering whether he was worth a try, but he walked straight past them towards the ticket-office.

Behind the broken glass, a girl was reading a magazine; she tore off the tickets without looking at him.

'What's the sea like?' asked Forte, peeling the money from his wallet.

'Fine,' she said, continuing to read.

Forte looked out over the bay; the sky was grey; in the distance white crests could be seen. 'Not beyond the red flag today!' Marta used to say to the girls when they were little.

As he pocketed his change he remembered how he had left Marta at the front door to their house, her eyes red from weeping and her face heavy with reproach. For the whole of that week which he had spent getting ready, up to the very last moment, she had fought to prevent this trip. With every means at her disposal: summoning her daughters, her sons-in-law and the family doctor in turn, trying to get them to dissuade him from leaving. Forte couldn't understand why his decision to go away with his daughter should have turned them all against him. It was as if they had made some mutual pact. They reproached him for the suffering this separation would cause the girl's mother; they told him that if anything, Federica needed to get away from the whole family; that he had decided to take her off on his own because he wanted to play the leading role and show them all up as incompetent. Forte was amazed by the vehemence with which they attacked him: he had never seen anything like it before.

'Play the leading role as usual.' What could have put such a thing into their heads? When had he ever given them cause to think such a thing? The opposite was true, if anything. He had always stood aside from matters.

Clearly there was more to it than that. Forte hadn't been able to understand exactly what.

Over the last few days his wife's mood had changed continually. Often she was unable to follow the thread of her thoughts through; she would break off in mid-sentence, keep it dangling for a few seconds, and then talk about something else as if the thought she'd set in motion had concluded itself in her mind and there was no longer any point in expounding it. Some mornings she woke up feeling cheerful, and talked of holiday plans, reproaching him for his selfishness in going to Ischia without her.

'I was the one who said we ought to go and clear things up there. I said so. It was my idea, and now you're going without me,' she would say, completely forgetting the reason for the trip and bursting into tears as soon as Forte reminded her.

'You think I don't care about my daughter,' she would then mumble between sobs.

Silvia and Caterina could hardly have failed to see the state their mother was in, and therefore what they should have done was try to make her see reason. But instead they backed her up. So Forte gave up trying to answer them; he let them talk and put up with their chorus of reproof. The only thing he bore in mind was the promise he had made to his daughter.

'Is the hydrofoil leaving straightaway?' he asked the girl hesitantly, not wanting to disturb her.

'Five minutes.'

He went back to the car. His son-in-law was waiting for him next to the cases. He had been sympathetic and tactful all through this business. The only one. Forte was grateful.

'Shall we wake her?'

'Yes, it's time we did. But just come with me for a second,' he said taking him by the arm.

'Shall we leave them here?' he said, pointing to the cases.

Forte glanced towards the two boys sitting on the ground. 'Hey!' he said. 'We're leaving the bags here, but we're coming straight back.'

The boys exchanged offended glances. 'We won't touch your bags. We sell cigarettes,' said the older boy in a superior tone.

'Exactly, I just wondered if you could keep an eye on them while we go off for a minute or two.'

The boys leapt to their feet. They took up their posts as sentinels.

The two men walked slowly along past the boats. They said nothing, listening to the water slapping, the buoys rubbing against the fenders, and the masts tinkling in the wind.

'If you could take it in turns to stay the night with Marta,' said Forte in a low voice, 'so that she's not left alone. That would be best. Or maybe you could persuade her to come and stay with you. She gets on with Silvia.'

'Don't worry. We'll see to it,' his son-in-law said reassuringly. 'Marta'll come and stay with us.'

'Thanks. Look, you know what a state Marta's been in these last few days. I had to leave. I was right to do so, I think.' He paused for a moment. 'Why is it Silvia doesn't realise the state Marta's in and say something to her?' Forte asked suddenly.

'She does realise, she realises perfectly well,' the younger man answered, with a note of strain in his voice.

'Then why doesn't she help me instead of attacking me? Why does she defend her?'

'I've wondered that too. We've argued over it. To tell the truth we've done nothing but argue; Federica's illness just seems to set us against each other.'

'Why?'

Silvia's husband didn't answer at once. Forte thought that he was embarrassed and maybe didn't want to discuss it.

'Don't worry,' he said. 'It'll pass. We're all upset at the moment.'

'No, it's not that,' he said heatedly. Forte realised that his son-in-law had been longing to talk to someone about it. 'Silvia didn't want you to leave with

123

Federica. She would have liked to take her place! She's always done everything with you in mind, even if she denies it.'

Forte had halted and was staring at him incredulously.

'It's true. Yesterday, without even realising, she said: "I've never gone anywhere with him. In our family you have to fall ill before anything happens." Everything's changed recently. Her calmness, the way she always said things were fine – well, it wasn't true. Now she attacks you, me, the children. If I mention you, she says that I want to split you from her, that I don't understand you or her. It's hell.'

Forte was dumbfounded. He felt that their every word and action was being stood on its head, and that he could no longer understand anything. 'I've been a normal father,' he said at last reluctantly, with the tone of an accused man before his judge. His words sounded comically inadequate. 'How could I have failed to realise? Yet I swear I wasn't living in another house.'

They both laughed and turned back.

'Do you think this trip will be of any use?' Forte asked him.

'I don't know, but you did right to come.'

'At least we'll leave you in peace for a while. You'll be better off without us.'

'There's that too,' he said smiling.

They stopped again.

'Sometimes I think it's all hopeless and it'll never end,' said Forte. 'But then there are times when I look at her and it just seems absurd that she should be like this, and I feel it can't go on much longer.'

'Yes, I keep changing my mind about it too.'

Forte looked out to sea. 'But anyway she wanted to make this trip. So even if it doesn't work out, it won't matter. It'll do her good.'

They went back to the boys and their cases. Forte held out a thousand lire to the elder one.

'You want a ticket?' the boy asked him at once, taking advantage of the intimacy achieved by this first transaction.

'Yes, why not, give me one.' He pocketed the ticket and gave him two more thousand-lire notes.

He opened the car door. Federica had just woken up.

'Right, let's get on board,' he said in a tone of exaggerated heartiness.

They helped her out. Forte slipped his arm under hers. Silvia's husband followed them with the cases. They walked in this fashion to the hydrofoil. On seeing them, a sailor came forward to help Federica aboard. He took her under the arm by force and they went slowly down the steps to the passenger cabin. Federica stopped at the first row of seats and sat down unhurriedly so that the other passengers wouldn't realise that she was unable to go any further. There were four other people. They were all islanders loaded up with packages. A woman and three men. They stared unembarrassedly at Federica, noting her awkwardness.

'I'll just go up and say goodbye,' Forte said to

her, as soon as he'd stowed the bags. He held a newspaper out to her. 'Do you want it?'

Federica clutched at it like a lifebelt and hid behind it. She darted quick glances over the top of the open page. The other passengers had gone back to talking about the sea and the next tourist season, paying no more attention to her.

The sailors slipped the ropes free, leapt aboard and pulled them up dripping.

'Take care of Marta,' said Forte standing at the top of the steps.

Silvia's husband made a reassuring gesture.

'I'll phone her as soon as we get there,' Forte shouted over the grinding throb of the engines, as the hydrofoil backed out and spray spattered over the deck.

Forte gave a last wave. He saw his son-in-law go off towards the car, and it was only then that he remembered that he hadn't thanked him. But it was too late now. He kept his eyes on him for a few seconds and then looked out to sea.

The hydrofoil had passed the end of the jetty and the first waves hit it sideways on, rocking it; then the craft rose above them. It began to slide forward on the water, smashing up and down in the troughs and crests of the sea.

'Will it be like this all the way to Ischia?' he asked a member of the crew.

'As far as Procida, then it'll get calmer.'

Forte went down to the cabin.

Fifteen

After Procida the sea was even rougher than before. Long crestless waves shook the hydrofoil. Inside the Ischitani talked about their own affairs, scarcely noticing the buffeting.

Every so often Federica looked up at the spray-spattered window. Forte talked to her about the house and what state it would be in, about the logs they would find chopped ready for the fire, about the wind that had uprooted a small peach-tree that had only recently been planted and other light topics that struck him as appropriate for the start of their trip together.

Now he fell silent for want of things to say. His wife used to claim that if it were up to him no important matters would ever get discussed. Forte wasn't fond of serious discussions; they never seemed true to him; ideas were private matters, to be kept tactfully to oneself. 'Disdainfully', his wife would say.

He looked at his daughter's hand resting next to his: it was as thin and pale as her face. It looked like an old woman's; the bluish veins stood out on the back.

'Here we go,' he thought. 'She's not talking. What

are we going to say to each other on our own?
What am I going to say to her?'

He looked at her unobtrusively. He feared her questioning gaze. One always had to have some remark
ready on one's lips. Despite her illness, she was beautiful. Forte wondered whether she seemed so beautiful
to other people. He tried to judge her objectively.
Her legs were long but not perfect. But then he
wasn't in favour of over-slender legs, the sophisticated
but charmless sort that one saw all the time in the
newspapers. Her simple pullover lent charm to her
face and to her dense black hair tied back behind
her shoulders. Her forehead was overhung by a short
fringe, tousled like a child's. He observed her black
eyebrows, her dark eyes with their bright white irises,
her small nose, and thick, half-open lips. Federica's
being was concentrated in her face. Her thin body
was just left to sprawl by itself on the chair, waiting
listlessly to be transported wherever it had to go.

'Maybe she doesn't strike other people as particularly beautiful.'

His thoughts were interrupted by a more violent
jolt than usual. The hydrofoil's engines slackened then
cut out. The craft sank down on the water to its
starting position.

Forte looked out of the port-hole: outside a line
of long waves was surging towards them. The second
impact was even more violent than the previous one.
The hydrofoil reeled to one side before crashing into
the hollow of the next wave. A few lifebelts rolled
down from the window-frames. Federica had closed

her eyes. They were being lifted upwards on an even higher crest. Another heavy thud, and then some other, less violent ones.

The hydrofoil's engines were started up again.

Forte looked at his daughter: she was still in the same position, with her eyes closed, her head leaning back on the head-rest. But her face was glistening with pain. She had her hand pressed to a specific point on her stomach.

'Are you in pain?' he asked her.

She shook her head. The hydrofoil started to judder again. With every crash, Federica pressed her hand against that same point, as if she wished to protect it from the blows.

'It's not possible . . .' thought Forte. 'We would have realised. She would have said. No, it's not possible,' he repeated to himself, while images of briefly glimpsed strangers and the faces of school-friends flickered across his mind.

He suddenly remembered their doctor's answer to his wife's question: 'A block due to her general condition.'

'No, it's not possible.'

Federica had opened her eyes again and was gazing at her father with a slight smile on her lips.

'Are you all right?' he asked.

Federica nodded, still smiling. 'Marco,' she thought, feeling happy for the first time after so long. 'Maybe I'm expecting a baby. Yes, maybe. Then I'll just have to find him.'

'And suppose she'd kept him hidden? But why?' he asked himself again, observing that strange smile.

'I'm going outside,' he said, getting up.

Standing on the deck of the hydrofoil, Forte watched the island getting larger. They had arrived. The red house on the promontory, the beaches round the little port. He saw his wife and his daughters waiting for him every Saturday night, with their tanned faces and their brightly-coloured clothes. He imagined climbing the steep road up to their house. But it wasn't like that. Federica was ill. Maybe she was expecting a baby. Nobody knew whose, nobody knew anything. What else had she been keeping from them? He tried once again to recall those school-friends who used to come and see her. There was one in particular. What was his name? Federica had gone out with him for a few years. No, it couldn't be him, he hadn't been round for ages. After she had started university, none of them had come back with her. Perhaps they met up outside. And who else was there? Federica never talked about anyone. She vaguely mentioned having friends, students on the same course as her, but they never came to the house. Why? He and Marta should have asked her before. But she was perfect. There was something beyond reproach about her life, her studies, what she wrote; her longing to travel; everything was normal, everything as it should be. And yet now there was this blank.

'No, she can't be pregnant,' he thought again, as the hydrofoil settled into the still water of the port, with the houses of pink stone along the front and the distant greenery rising up to the mountain in the centre of the island.

Sixteen

'I'll be back in a minute or two,' he told her through the bathroom door after helping her into the bath.

On his way down the stairs, he wondered how he was going to help her get dressed and undressed without making her feel uncomfortable and without feeling so himself.

He had looked her over quickly while she was still in her underwear. Her body was bony and unshapely. She could hardly be pregnant. Anyway he mustn't mention it to anyone, least of all to his wife. Marta would come at once. He was already worried that she might come in any case.

He went downstairs to the kitchen. The woman who helped out in the summer was preparing dinner.

'How are things, Adele?' he asked her as he entered.

'Fine, everything's fine,' she said laconically.

She was twenty-two and had three children. Hers was a young girl's face above a body made flabby by pregnancies.

'And how's your husband?'

'Fine. He's got a job at the hotel. He's staying here this year.'

'And the children?'

'Fine, all three of them. Another one due in five months.'

Forte's eyes opened wide. This was singularly pertinent news. 'And when are you going to stop?' he said, trying to smile.

'This is the last one,' she said, laughing.

Four months pregnant and no sign of it. The news dispirited him.

'Do you want me every day?' she asked, continuing to wash the vegetables.

'Yes, that would be best. If you could come early in the morning, then you could help her get dressed and prepare something to eat. My wife is likely to phone frequently. Tell her everything's fine.'

'What's wrong with her?' she said, looking straight at him.

'She's not well. But she'll soon get back to shape here.'

'She should take the mud-baths, they're good for everything.'

'Can I come in?' came a man's voice from the top of the stairs.

'It's Nicoló,' she said, blushing. There had been something between her and the gardener many years before and she still blushed every time she pronounced his name.

'I'm coming,' Forte said, climbing back up the stairs.

When he saw him at the door, with his beret on his head and his eight-year-old son by his side, he experienced the same joy as ever and he felt saved from all these women's problems. Forte considered Nicoló as a kind of alter-ego – an alter-ego in the role of a gardener. Sometimes he felt that Nicoló's job actually made him superior. There was nothing vague or wasteful about his work. He was an extremely handsome man: lean, dark-haired and blue-eyed. He talked and smiled very little. But they understood each other well; they thought along the same lines. Now, as always, they would discuss the trim little world of his garden.

'Good afternoon, Nicoló. How are things?'

'Afternoon,' he replied.

'Afternoon,' said the boy in exactly the same way as his father.

'I brought the wood, the driest pieces. I put it next to the fireplace,' he said, going straight to the point. 'The wind blew everything down this year.' He indicated the garden with his hand.

'I know,' said Forte. 'The peach-tree and what else?'

He called Adele and told her to go and help Federica. He went out into the garden.

Nicoló's son had grown as lean as his father. Forte looked at the boy's slender legs. And in his place he saw that son he had never had himself, running after him in the garden. A boy in short trousers, with dark eyes like Federica's. With him everything would have been easier perhaps. He would have brought him along too, just like Nicoló.

They halted in front of a flowerbed with hydrangeas and wind-curved wayfaring-trees.

'Do you like flowers too?' Forte asked the shy child.

'He doesn't like anything,' his father grumbled, watching the boy kick a clod of earth. 'Except shopping, like his mother.'

The boy had lowered his head, smiling at these same old words. Forte turned and listened to Nicoló's account of the wayfaring-trees.

While Nicoló talked, he suddenly thought that maybe all fathers imagined some unborn child and never succeeded in being fathers to those they actually had.

'If we want to do things properly,' the gardener was saying, 'I reckon we ought to start all over again. There's nothing worth saving here.' He pulled up a hydrangea root. 'Everything needs replanting.'

'And what shall we replace it with? The wayfaring-trees have gone rotten. Let's make it all hydrangeas.'

'Geraniums and marguerites, like those over there,' said Nicoló, walking towards another part of the garden and pointing to an array of terraced flowerbeds that flanked the steps into the garden.

Everything was in perfect order: straightened and trimmed to the very last weed, the earth smoothed over and the flowers in neat rows and separated from the tiles and stone of the walls. Everything grew in its place. An orderly little kingdom ruled over by Nicoló.

'He knows so many things and yet he isn't able to make other people love them. Isn't able to or doesn't want to?' he suddenly wondered, seeing the precision with which Nicoló pulled up a tiny blade of frail, pale-green grass that had grown in a crack, eluding his attention.

The boy had stopped a little farther on. He seemed to Forte to be eyeing his father with hostility.

'Yes,' he said. 'All right. We'll plant geraniums and marguerites. And in place of the peach-tree I'd like to buy a small palm.'

He turned back towards the house. He wanted to find out how Federica was.

'A palm-tree?' said Nicoló in surprise, following him.

'Yes, a palm-tree.'

'And what about when it grows?' he asked ironically.

'Well, it'll grow, Nicoló. I'll go and look for one tomorrow with my daughter. We could meet then to work out the accounts as well,' he said, re-entering the house.

Federica was lying on the sofa next to the fireplace. It was a small room with a simple fireplace in white stone, sofas around the hearth and a dining-table in one corner. In the summer they were always outside and they rarely came at any other time of the year.

The house was not large or splendid. Forte didn't earn enough for a grand villa; and neither he nor his wife loved luxury. It was a small villa on a hill, nestling amidst the greenery along with eight other houses. The builder had given each house the name of a muse. Federica, Caterina and Silvia had learnt them all by heart. Federica smiled slightly; at school once, she had amazed her teacher by reciting all the names of the muses.

Those days were not so long in the past. But now, as she thought about what was happening to her, about Marco and her illness, she was unable to pinpoint any dates in her childhood. It was all a vague, muddled blur, from which an occasional moment might emerge, but no clear memory. Thus, when she tried to link some sensation to a particular date or to a particular age, she felt as if she were being whirled in a vortex, which reduced her to a body without memories, lying on a sofa. And so she stopped trying to fix things precisely, and allowed her thoughts to wander where they would, grasping only at those that had some connection with Marco: they were the most unlikely ones, the ones most people would have doubted, and for this reason they struck her as being the closest to reality. She struggled to remember tiny things that had happened between them in order to try and reconstruct longer periods of time. Occasionally she thought they had been together a year, sometimes a month. The days all resembled one another and the slight variants she managed to spot could have been those that marked a day in a month or a month in a year. No strata had been laid down as in her other adolescent friendships. At the end of the affair they knew each other no more or less than they had on the first day. Each of them had assimilated the other. They had been jostled by the crowd into the one free corner of a bus full of excited, incomprehensible people. They had held hands and had got off at the other end without needing to say anything to each other, merely to decide who would buy the cigarettes and who the drinks.

First it had been the wall outside the university, then Marco's room at the *pensione* Aurora – no-man's-land where they felt they had been born and had grown up together. Each time they said goodbye they were instantly erased from the other person's life. Federica found that the best way to have Marco with her was to touch some part of her body and reflect on it. If she looked at her foot, at once his own feet came to mind, and she recalled how they would measure them up against one another and how he would lock them round her neck, slither them down her body and her sides, slide them under her arms, and pull her towards him.

'Are you hungry?' her father asked, standing in front of the sofa, watching her.

Federica started and opened her eyes. She at once shook her head to hide her thoughts. Forte observed her.

'Nothing to drink either?' he asked, remembering how the doctors had advised them not to force her to eat.

Federica nodded.

'Water, wine or beer?'

Federica didn't reply. Forte remembered the game they used to play in summer when only one question could be asked at a time because they were only allowed to answer yes or no.

'Water?'

Federica nodded. Forte went into the kitchen and returned with a tray of food prepared by Adele. He handed her the glass of water.

'You don't mind if I eat?'

Federica had pulled herself up and now gazed at him listlessly. Forte settled himself in the armchair and started eating. Federica continued to stare at him with the same impenetrable expression.

'I told Nicoló that I want to plant a palm-tree. Let's go and buy it tomorrow, shall we?'

Federica smiled without answering. Forte recognised the smile as the one she used when making fun of some fixation of his.

'Why are you laughing? Don't you like palm-trees?'

Federica smiled again.

'I didn't say that's all we'd do tomorrow. What would you like to do? Go to the beach, if it doesn't rain?'

Federica nodded without conviction. Forte started eating again. He decided not to ask her too many questions. He searched his mind for some other topic. It was incredible how hard it was to talk without asking questions.

'I told them at the office I'd be away for a week. But we can stay longer. After all I've taken very few holidays.'

Incredible how all he could think of was business matters.

'Listen. Don't you feel like writing any more?'

138

Federica shook her head.

'But you used to write such a lot. You used to keep a diary, didn't you?'

Federica suddenly looked scared and nodded. Forte realised that she didn't want to think about the diary and felt that he ought to insist.

'Did you bring it with you?'

Federica hesitated before replying, then nodded.

'To write or to read through? What would happen, do you think, if I were to read it? Do you write a lot of secret things?'

Federica looked at her father in a sulky fashion and shook her head.

'I didn't say I *wanted* to read it, I'd never do that. Diaries are written not to be read by other people. Or maybe because one hopes that sooner or later someone will read them. Would you like me to read it?'

Federica shook her head. She closed her eyes. Forte said nothing and continued to eat for a while in silence.

'Let's play the game where you have to guess a character,' he said suddenly.

Federica opened her eyes in surprise.

'You think of someone and I'll ask the questions. Obviously you can't talk, or it doesn't count.'

Federica pulled an ironic face. Forte smiled.

'OK, have you thought?'

Federica nodded.

'Is it a man?'

She shook her head.

'Is it an important woman? A public figure?'

No.

'Just someone we know then?'

Yes.

'Someone in our family?'

Yes.

'And I don't know her well?'

No.

Forte observed her, put the tray down and lit a cigarette. He inhaled, keeping his eyes on her. His daughter looked at him with a sly expression.

'A woman in the family whom I don't know well.'

Yes.

'I've got four women in the house. One of the four I don't know well. Or all four.'

Federica let out a silent giggle which struck both of them as extremely comic.

Forte burst out laughing. Federica lifted her hand with one finger raised.

'I can ask just one more question?'

Yes.

'Is there a man in your life?' he asked, suddenly looking at her. Federica nodded quickly, and looked away from her father.

'So it's not you.'

Federica didn't answer.

'Oh, of course, you can't answer any more questions,' he said.

'She'll lie,' thought Forte. 'Now she'll change the name she's thought of. She'll try to cheat me just as she used to when she was small and changed the rules.'

'It's you,' he said firmly, continuing to look at her.

Federica raised her eyes to her father.

'He wouldn't believe me and anyway he couldn't understand,' she thought before answering.

She shook her head.

'So I've lost,' he said. 'I'll try and guess. Was it Silvia?'

Federica nodded absently. She was once again impenetrable and listless.

'Was she lying or not?' wondered Forte.

Seventeen

The garden was in darkness. Forte pulled the shutters towards himself: the trees were rocked by the wind, which was heavy with rain. As he closed the shutters he felt a sudden desire to leave. He thought of his wife back home and of his days marked by the steady rhythm of work. On the phone his wife tried to keep her voice bright, in an effort to hide her anxiety. She had gone to stay with Silvia. She was all right, she said sadly, it was his daughter he should think of. He wished she were there to help him, to put herself between him and their daughter as always. He was afraid of the days ahead.

He closed the living-room shutters and sat down in the armchair again. He picked up the book from the floor. Federica was asleep on the sofa. She hadn't eaten, she kept falling asleep and dreaming, since he could see her twitching in her sleep. Every so often she would awaken with a start and her eyes would roam in search of him. Forte had picked out one of the books from the living-room: holiday-books, that had been read or half-read on the beach and were crusted with sand and salt. An odd collection, which had accumulated haphazardly, consisting of books brought there by each of them and then forgotten: fairy-tales, detective-stories and curiosities; some of them complete, others in tatters, lacking pages and covers, the paper torn or shrivelled by sea-water, whole chapters without any order or sense, all jumbled together like objects at a flea-market.

For a few seconds he had forced his eyes along the lines. But his mind kept halting at single words, refusing to make associations. So he had given up reading and, with his eyes resting on the cover, had let his mind wander aimlessly. It wasn't natural to him. Most people were a prey to confused ideas and irrationality. But if one's desire was to understand, it was essential not to be involved.

'But understanding is also being involved,' he at once thought, from his habit of contradicting every statement he made and testing its meaning by its opposite. 'This is also true. But understanding is above all the capacity to judge things critically, with detachment. For example: if one doesn't want dictatorships, one must never be seduced by their outward shows. Never be moved by military marches. No goose-flesh on hearing the wedding-march that accompanies the dictator's daughter on her way up to the altar. Judging means not being seduced and remaining detached.'

He thought of the many moments in his life when it had been easy for him to understand and judge a situation better than other people, to keep it under control without allowing himself to get involved.

'But if one is never moved by military parades then one can't understand the fascination they exert over other people. Exactly. That is true too, like its opposite. Understanding the killer means having killed yourself. No, let's not take it too far. It means having imagined doing so once. He took the sins of the world upon himself and took them away. It can't be done.' He smiled silently.

His book slipped to the floor. In her sleep Federica stretched her legs out to the end of the sofa and half-lifted her face from where it lay buried in the cushion.

'She can't be expecting a baby. She would have talked about it. Suppose it were true? Why should she have concealed it? We would have found a sol-ution.' He felt chilled as he thought of someone Federica might have kept hidden. Who could this unknown person be, whom Federica had not wanted to talk about?

'It's not possible.' He tried to drive away the idea of the intruder. 'The others had their love-affairs and got married, and they talked about them. So why should she . . . ? No, it's not possible.'

He lit a cigarette. He found himself once more immersed in the anguish of those days. He ran his mind over the doctors' opinions and the family dis-cussions; and each time the idea of the stranger loomed up and overshadowed all other considerations. He asked himself yet again what reasons Federica could have had for saying nothing. And these questions all seemed so absurd that he persuaded himself that it wasn't possible, and then a second later that it might be.

'We'll have to find out,' he thought, stubbing the cigarette out fiercely in the ash-tray. 'And how? She won't talk. The diary —' It flashed into his mind as if suggested by someone else. 'Read another person's diary. Impossible. But she probably wrote something in the diary. And suppose the truth were contained there?'

He lit another cigarette. The thought of reading her diary while she was asleep attracted and repelled him at the same time. He tried to marshal all his convictions on an action of this sort.

'The idea of truth can never justify intruding on another person's secret. It's always wrong to use force, whatever the aim. It's not admissible to resort to trickery to find out something that someone doesn't wish to say. Right, and that means we shouldn't do anything to get her to talk.'

He looked at his daughter asleep.

'Maybe it's wrong to read an adult's diary, but with a sick girl, one should. No, there's no difference. It's the principle that counts.'

He looked at her again and he felt it was dishonest to cheat her. She was like a child, asleep with her fist clenched and her mouth half-open. She seemed to be asking for help.

'But maybe I ought to intervene, I ought to read it. No, I've got no right. First of all, there's no guarantee that what's written there will help me to understand her illness. There might also be some personal interest on my part to read what she's written. And in that case it would just be curiosity. And anyway, even if there were some useful information, I'd read several other private things that she has every right to keep from me and from other people. It's not admissible. There are no such things as principles valid in certain situations and not in others. I must respect her even if she's sick at the moment,' he told himself energetically to put an end to his doubts. He tried not to think about it, but without success.

'Of course many people would behave differently.' Against his will, he found himself listening to other voices, other arguments, hypotheses and pleas.

'There's no such thing as a lasting understanding any more. Nothing can be grasped for more than a few seconds at a time.'

He picked his book up again and let his eyes wander round the dimly lit room.

'If only one could relax and just for once go beyond one's own confines, one's usual lines of reasoning. If only it were possible to be different from one's usual self for once.'

He looked up to the top of the staircase. That was where his daughters used to emerge each morning, still wearing their nightdresses. He always woke up first and would sit in the armchair holding a book, just as he was doing now. With their hair tousled and their eyes bleary they would glance out of the windows and their faces would brighten at the sight

of the sun and the thought of the beach; then a
second later they would spot him.

One day he had walked along the water's edge
holding Federica's hand; she was perhaps seven at
the time. The other two were with their mother
under the beach-umbrella.

Federica's hand in his.

'What do you do when I'm not here?' he had
asked her.

'I wait for you to come.'

'I'll bet! You get up to all sorts of things. Don't
you like staying with Mamma and your sisters?'

'Yes.'

'And so?'

'What do you do when I'm not there?'

'I work.'

'What do you do?'

'Lots of things. There are lots of people who work
with me. We all have to decide whether to give
money or not to companies and to people who ask
for it and then use it to make things.'

'What do they make?'

'Lots of things. Things to eat, cars, toys, boats . . .'

'And do they work as well?'

'Yes, of course, they all work. So, what do you
do when I'm in Rome working?'

'I swim, play a bit, wait for you to come.'

Forte leaned back in the armchair, closed the book
and then his eyes. Federica's voice as a child echoed
in his mind like a tiny bell, tinkling ever more faintly.

'But I didn't swim this week. There were waves

and I didn't play much either. The waves were so high that I'd have drowned. So Mamma said I could only go in close to the shore. The red flag was out. Why do they put it there?'

'To show that it's dangerous.'

'But anyone can see that the sea's rough.'

'But some silly person might want to go in all the same and so they put it out to warn him. You would have gone in if the flag hadn't been there.'

'Yes.' She looked at her father and laughed. 'But I'm little, how am I supposed to know?'

'She's little,' thought Forte drowsing, while his thoughts and the voices from the past mingled in an ageless and timeless concerto. 'My daughter, the littlest one.'

Against his will, tears surged behind his lowered eyelids.

'No more thinking. No more thoughts. How can one possibly tell what one ought to do, with all these thoughts that keep coming? One should stop thinking and finally understand. Understand what?' he suddenly asked himself, as sleep obscured all lasting comprehension.

'Understand what can't be understood by thought alone.'

This silent assertion struck him as being right and reassuring. There was no need to think about anything, no need to strain himself; he could sleep.

Eighteen

Their first week on Ischia was over. They had bought the palm-tree for the garden; they had walked along the grey, wintry beach; they had visited the port to do their shopping; Forte had bought her books, pens and notepads to encourage her to write.

They had taken up walking along the beach again. Every day he was presented with the problem of what to get her to do. As the days went by, Forte asked himself what point there was in continually wandering around an island he knew to the last square inch, and wondered whether it might not have been better to stay at home and try to get her to talk or to talk to her himself. But what he feared most now was his daughter's sombre stare and those thoughts that assailed him the moment he tried to work out the best way of tackling her illness. These thoughts were automatically triggered off by any chance meeting of their eyes, by even a single glance of Federica's in his direction. Every day he phoned his wife and told her how they were spending their time.

Now and again, without going into the matter too deeply, he reflected on the fact that it was the first time they had ever been on a trip together. And Federica was the daughter he was closest to; yet he was not at ease with her by himself. Their solitude embarrassed him, made him feel uncomfortable; he didn't know how to behave. He realised that it was a long time since he'd been alone with anyone.

After those first few days he had ceased to speculate on a possible secret in his daughter's life.

It was evening again, an evening no different from all the others. Federica had eaten hardly anything. Now she was stretched on the sofa with her face pale and drawn, her expression as unfathomable as ever. Her real beauty still lay in her long black hair tied behind her neck, and the short fringe that just tickled her forehead. Her hands were fiddling and every so often she gnawed her finger-nails.

'You're not bored?' he asked.

'No,' she indicated.

'I am,' said Forte, losing his temper. 'We can't go on like this. I can't think of any more questions to ask you and I don't know what to say to you.'

She didn't react. Forte stood up suddenly and started pacing to and fro.

'Maybe I'm not patient enough. But how can I help you if you won't say anything? I see you lying there for no reason, you won't eat and you can hardly walk. And I can't do anything for you . . . Why don't you answer?'

He paused in front of her.

'Look, you know I don't want to use any violence. I can't treat you like a hopeless child. Whatever else, I want to respect you. I could send you off to a clinic. You'd be forced to eat there and they'd give you their own kind of treatment. The doctors disapprove of me, they all think I was wrong to bring you here. So does Mamma. And now I have to admit they were right. Do you understand what I'm saying?'

Federica nodded.

'So why won't you help me? You don't even want to write. You don't want to do anything!' This last sentence came out imploringly.

Federica continued to stare at her hands.

'Listen to me.' He sat down next to her. 'I left the office, but that doesn't matter. Everything's going to pieces there, I don't care. I really believed you wanted to come away with me. And I wanted to come with you. And now I'm very glad to be here with you.' He lied without looking her in the eyes. 'But there's got to be some point to all this. You must get better and take up your life again.' He looked at her again. 'I know you want to get better.'

He waited for a moment to see some reaction in her. But Federica's face was imperturbable.

'Listen. I think you're intelligent, very intelligent. And you're mature too. Without any doubt more mature than most people your age. What I mean is, everything was fine before!' He was getting worked up. 'You were happy. You did a lot of things. What's wrong or abnormal in your life? I can't see anything. The way I see it, you're beautiful, intelligent, you've got all kinds of possibilities. What's wrong then? Is there something wrong?'

Federica shook her head.

'So? What's the reason for all this? Did something happen to you?'

With a firm movement of her head, as if she had to overcome some resistance, Federica nodded. Forte felt his heart miss two beats.

'So something happened to you that I don't know about?' he asked, hoping for one moment that this clarificatory event did not exist.

Federica nodded again.

'And why have you never said so before? You knew about it?'

Federica shook her head.

'What? But you know now?'

Federica shook her head again.

'You don't? How can that be? You know something happened to you but you don't know what? You can't remember anymore?'

Federica shook her head. Forte tried to keep calm, to reflect on the next question.

'But you must know something, some fact that can put me on the right track?'

Federica lowered her head.

'You don't want to say? You could write it for me . . .'

Federica thought for a moment and then nodded uncertainly.

Forte got up, opened a drawer with shaking hands, and took out a notepad and pen.

Federica took the pen in her fingers, opened the pad, stared for a second at the blank sheet and then, with the trembling hand of an old woman, wrote just one crooked word in the centre of the page.

Forte looked at the page, at the word written there, and was unable to speak.

'Who is Marco?' he mumbled at last, his tone mechanical.

Federica gave a barely perceptible shrug. It could have been a gesture of apathy and boredom. But it wasn't. It was so out of place and so unexpected that it was frightening.

'You don't know?'

Federica shook her head and looked at her father, her eyes inexpressibly sad.

Forte felt as if he were intruding for the first time into the life of a woman that neither of them knew; a woman with a story that could be told, a story containing a character named Marco with whom the woman at some point had had some kind of re-lationship – friendship or love; they had met in some house or walked the streets together. In an instant all kinds of possible stories came to mind. All kinds of stories and none.

'You don't remember?'

Federica shook her head and burst into a choked lament. She buried her face in her hands. It was the first time he had heard her voice in ages. But that lament struck him as embarrassing. He felt no compassion for her. He merely hoped that it was all untrue.

'It's not possible,' he thought. 'What does she mean, she doesn't know anything? Who is he? And how can she tell me now the name of someone she knows nothing about? It makes no sense. Maybe she's inventing and none of it's true. She said it just to help me find something. Yes, maybe that's it. She doesn't know herself what she ought to say. She's sick. I'm making a mistake in asking her all these questions. Yet I shouldn't miss this chance of her opening up to me.'

Federica kept her face between her hands. Forte stretched his hand out to caress her, but couldn't bring himself to touch her.

'Where did you meet him?'

She took her hands from her face; it was streaked with tears.

'At the university?'

'He'll never believe me. He can't imagine. What shall I say to him? I don't know anything now,' she thought, looking at him.

'Maybe she's taken it into her head that I want to send her to a clinic. She's frightened and she's just said the first thing that came into her head. Yes, it must be that,' he thought.

'He'll never understand. I mustn't say anything.'

'I mustn't ask her too many questions.'

'I never had any intention of sending you to a clinic, you know?' he said with a reassuring smile. 'Was that what you were afraid of?'

Federica gazed at him for a long while, then dried her eyes and nodded without looking at him.

Forte gave her a rapid caress.

'Now lie back and keep calm. I don't like to see you this way.'

He made her lie down on the sofa. He sat in the armchair some distance from her and smiled at her again.

'You find it hard to remember why you've been ill. When you're better, you'll remember everything. Now you mustn't strain yourself,' he said at last with a tremor in his voice which she immediately noticed.

Federica nodded. Her eyes, as they gazed at her father, were cold now.

'You should re-read your diary. It might help you, thinking over what you wrote when you were well,' he said, lighting a cigarette.

He hesitated for a moment before asking her the question he had in mind.

'Did you write anything about this Marco in your diary?'

Federica shook her head at once.

'And why didn't you write anything?'

He looked at her, awaiting her answer. But Federica didn't have one. She didn't know why she'd never written about him; who had torn the pages from the diary, or why. Now she didn't even know how they had met.

'I must remember. I must try and understand what happened,' she thought as she felt the tears surging again. She closed her eyes so that he shouldn't see.

'Don't tire yourself now. You'll remember every-thing when you're better. There's no point in straining

155

yourself. What you need now is to pull yourself together and get better, OK?'

Federica agreed automatically.

'And if it takes time, we'll stay here as long as necessary. Everything will turn out all right, you'll see.'

He fell silent. He inhaled his smoke and smiled at her.

'Do you feel better now?' he asked, feeling better himself. 'Shall we see what's on television? We've never turned it on yet. Let's see if it's working or if the damp has done for it.'

Federica watched him fuss around with the aerial. 'He doesn't want to know anything about it. Why not?'

She had to be wary of him as well. Yes, what she had to do was get better and remember. Involuntarily she brought air up from her lungs; the little tongue clammed up at the back of her throat as ever.

The television worked. She quickly dried a tear as he turned.

'There's a film on,' he said, moving towards the sofa. 'Do you want to watch it? It might take us out of ourselves for a while. What do you say?'

He caressed her hair rapidly, absently.

Nineteen

A nother week had gone by without any results. 'I must keep her occupied and make her move,' he had thought at the beginning of the week. 'First of all she must recover her strength and not give in to this senseless torpor. If she just lies around, she'll never feel hungry and never find the energy to get better. Less thinking, more action. The illness all comes from this continual introspection.'

So Forte had kept her on the move all day long; although the island was full of interesting spots and walks, it now seemed small and limited to them. He had not achieved his aim of making her recover her strength and her desire to eat and talk. Federica followed him docilely, she walked, sat down, gazed at things and strolled along the beach, but she did it all so placidly and with such resignation that even as she walked she managed to appear motionless; and everything about her remained obscure and silent.

Bosio phoned from the office every day now. To fill him in on things, he said. Actually, Forte's absence was beginning to weigh on him. He had coped very well, everybody said; and he himself felt more confident and intelligent. Not quite like the others perhaps, but almost. At the end of the second week, however, he started to feel worried. He realised that the presence of his boss was as indispensable to him as his morning coffee.

'I don't know when I'll be able to return. Things are improving, she feels better, but she's not right yet,' he had answered him on the phone, just as he repeated to his wife every day. 'Another week or maybe two. Yes, two at the most.'

Bosio didn't know what the matter was with Forte's daughter. Forte had spoken about it only vaguely: an attack of depression, something to do with her age. But Bosio guessed there was something more mysterious and serious.

'Drugs perhaps,' he murmured to Forte's secretary with the respect due to a famous illness.

'Poor man, him as well,' she answered, echoing his tone and at once listing all the cases she knew of.

'Come here for a couple of days, we can take all the necessary decisions and you can go back to Rome,' Forte said to him on the phone at last.

Bosio agreed at once. He was curious to meet this girl who had made the inflexible Forte give way, obliging him to take a holiday out of season – Forte who never even took one in August. Bosio would be there in two days.

That morning Forte had decided they would ascend Mount Epomeo. It was one of the ritual walks he used to take when his daughters were children. They usually did it in September, after rain. From the mountain, on the first clear day after storms, one could see the sharp outlines of the nearby islands: Capri, Procida, Ventotene, sometimes Ponza. At the top there was a shelter where they would go and drink wine, while waiting for the sun to set. Sometimes they would decide to stay and sleep in the little rooms of the shelter, which resembled monks' cells. Usually they would go back down in the darkness. Forte always preferred to return. There was no phone in the shelter; and anyway, on Sunday he had to get back to Rome. His daughters would secretly pour wine out for him while he was looking out to sea, to make him forget the time. Later they themselves lost interest. They knew by heart the names of the islands and the headlands; they knew the narrow road that wound its way up the steep slopes of the mountain; the precipice of volcanic rocks reached by a narrow path overhanging the void. They had grown up.

It was a cold, windy morning. While Forte was taking his coffee, Adele advised him not to go.

'You could get blown off. Especially Federica, who's lighter than a feather,' she said, in the placid tone she always adopted to depict dramas and disasters.

From the living-room window they could see the young trees in the garden bent low by the violent gusts of wind.

'It's too windy, it won't rain,' thought Forte sipping his coffee.

'Tell her to take her anorak,' he said to Adele, running upstairs to his room.

At the bottom of the dark wooden wardrobe he found his walking-boots wrapped in newspaper. There were swimming-costumes, sandals, and beach-wraps too: a smell of sea-salt and wood. Everything had been arranged carefully by his wife. He glanced at the bed, unmade only on one side. He thought of those summer nights when he fell asleep next to her tanned body. Saturday and Sunday evenings; the rest of the week he worked in Rome. His wife pitied him because he could never take a holiday. He let her pity him. He knew that by Sunday evening or at the latest Monday morning, when he caught the hydrofoil, his feeling would be one of inner satisfaction at the knowledge that he was returning to the troops of pitied workers. Two or three days of holiday were quite enough. During the August holiday week, their house would fill with friends with whom he always ended up talking about work, and thus he was saved. But he let her pity him. He would never have wished her to know his real thoughts. She would have felt betrayed. No longer would she have greeted him with that same real joy, no longer would she have waited for him at the port, her daughters by her side. And when he stood on the deck of the hydrofoil, watching as each throb of the engines brought her into clearer focus, he himself felt a real happiness that he would never have wished to relinquish – the same happiness that he felt when he embraced her in bed after a week of absence. But for all this to be real, it could only last a weekend. No longer. Marriage was like that. Or he was like that. Anyway she must never know.

'I wonder whether she's ever realised,' he said to himself, throwing a last glance at the bed before going into the bathroom.

He started to shave in front of the mirror, recalling the departures and arrivals of which his holidays consisted.

'Maybe I'm the one who's never realised all sort of things,' he reflected, scraping the razor over his cheek and flicking the white foam into the water. 'Yes, maybe that's it,' he repeated to himself, thinking back to one of his arrivals, many years ago.

Nobody had been waiting for him that evening. He had said that he wouldn't be able to get away. But in the end he had managed it. He had arrived on the last steamer. He came down the garden steps and, halting half-way down, listened to their laughter. Female laughter.

'How many women are there this evening?' he had wondered, coming down noiselessly.

He could see them now, while remaining unseen himself. There were a great many people: his daughters' friends, his wife's sisters and friends. They were playing cards at several tables spread out all over the garden. There were cakes and drinks, and everyone was happy and intent on having a good time. There was nothing wrong with that. He looked at her: her fair hair was drawn back, her neck and face tanned; her neck was as smooth and round as a child's despite her forty years. She was laughing and leaning slightly over towards her neighbour's cards; he was an insignificant-looking man, one of those types with a permanent suntan, who are always on holiday. They were laughing and their faces were very close. There was nothing wrong with that. Forte knew it. And yet her cheerfulness and the party atmosphere grated on him.

'It's probably like this every evening when I'm not here,' he thought. 'It's not a special evening.'

'Papà!' one of his daughters shouted, the first to see him hiding behind the window.

His wife came towards him, her face slightly flushed and her eyes dancing, but there was something about her that he didn't recognise.

'That's what she's like without me. They're all so happy,' he thought as he embraced her.

He shaved slowly and that thought from the past returned together with other memories: 'What do you do when I'm not here? – I wait for you to come.'

That evening in bed he had held her in his arms for longer than usual.

What did they do when he wasn't there? What did their enjoyment consist of? It wasn't the same when they enjoyed themselves with him. Why not?

'They waited for me so eagerly at the port. No doubt of it,' he reassured himself, sliding the razor delicately over his neck.

'But they . . . well, who really knows them? Nobody. It's a fact. They're all the same. Full of quirks. Irrational, illogical. Their behaviour's irrational and unfathomable.' He rinsed the razor in the washbasin and then, with even greater precision, as if he wanted his gesture to be in complete contrast with the irrationality of his women, he began to pass it over those areas still white with cream.

'I thought it was a cliché. But it's also true. They're unfathomable. Of course everything's a bit like that nowadays. But at least we know why we do something. That much at least. But then perhaps not. Maybe they know better. Or maybe nobody knows. Everything and anything is possible.' He stood there with his razor poised in the air. That last thought had thought itself.

'Of course everything and anything is possible.' He started shaving again. 'So what?'

Once again he halted his razor in mid-air. These thoughts were his usual ones. Yet now they no longer seemed the same.

'Everyone has his own truths. His own thoughts. And there are so many reasons, so many thoughts, so many . . .' He tried to shave without thinking.

He passed his hand over his face to remove the rest of the soap. He stared into the mirror. With one firm press he unplugged the wash-basin.

His hand, still holding the razor, began to tremble slightly. Forte stared at the hand: it was trembling, but his arm was still. He put the razor down on the side of the wash-basin. The tremor increased. He gripped the hand with the other one. He looked at his face in the mirror: his eyes were red-rimmed, his lower lip fixed in a grimace.

'It never used to be like that,' he thought, looking at himself. 'I never used to be like that. Why? I was also less intelligent.'

A thought that was at once strange and familiar followed hard upon this last one. He didn't immediately recognise it.

'*Memories become anecdotes and youthful emotions seem like legends.*' What was it? Something he had read? Where? He suddenly remembered. He had forgotten all about it. A story. A story he'd written. When?

He sat on the side of the bath, crossing his legs under his dressing-gown. He had been twenty at the time. He wrote short stories. It wasn't a question of style: he couldn't manage anything longer.

It was a time of his life when he was always quarrelling with his father. He used to buy jazz records and he wanted to be an architect. In his room he would listen to Charlie Parker and mentally design a world which was both rational and free – stripped to the essentials like the materials used by the Bauhaus architects. Even now, as he thought back to it, he found it beautiful. He had been right to preserve this concept in his mind all these years. As he had grown older he had ceased to believe in all the things he had stood up for so vociferously against his father; none the less they were the ideas of his youth, and they had been preserved silent and intact in his consciousness. They were no longer good in the sense of being right. It wasn't a question of facts any more. They were free from any test of truth, but he couldn't throw them off.

With his head resting against the wall above the bath, Forte observed his hand settle to a gradual calm. He felt that those distant ideas, denied by the facts of his life, were the only ideas left to him. Whatever he had chosen or done since then depended perhaps on those tattered, dog-eared books which he used to re-read every evening and annotate in the margins and between the lines, until his own writing blurred into the printed text. Everything in them had seemed like a discovery to him. Many years later, flicking through the yellowing pages, before stowing them away on a new shelf in a new house, he had realised that the statements he had marked with rows of question-marks were not in fact obscure at all. He had laughed and wondered why on earth he hadn't understood them at the time.

All the books he had bought in later years had been arranged in alphabetical order – all except those. They had all remained together, united by the period of his life in which he had read them.

'Like the books left here,' he thought, standing up and staring at his face in the mirror. 'Maybe that's how it was with them too. Anyway nothing came of it all,' he said impatiently, fed up with these memories.

'The truth is that it was all wrong. The Bauhaus was wiped out by Nazism. Charlie Parker was killed by an overdose.' He turned on the tap and rinsed his face; then he looked at himself in the mirror again.

He had a good many wrinkles. But the important thing was to stay fresh mentally. Nothing else counted. This whole business would soon be cleared up, because Federica was the most intelligent of them all, the smartest. It had just been a brief skid off the rails, and it would soon be put right. Just so long as he could keep his thoughts clear.

He went back into the bedroom to get dressed. Every so often he looked out of the window distractedly and saw the bent trees and the black clouds on the horizon.

Twenty

They walked up the slope side by side. Forte held his daughter under her arm. A village boy followed hard on their heels.

The weather had deteriorated yet further. Every so often the boy glanced up at them, wondering if they really wanted to continue the climb in these conditions.

Federica's hair was tied back in a long pony-tail that hung straight down her back; the wind stirred only the short-trimmed curls on her forehead and her neck. Despite the fact that the path, scraggy with rocks and bushes, was getting steeper and narrower with every step they took, Federica held her head straight and still as if the climb required no effort on her part.

'Whenever you get tired we can stop,' Forte said, feeling tired himself. 'You mustn't strain yourself.'

Federica shrugged slightly.

'You remember? All those trips we've made up here?'

Federica nodded and gave a tiny faded smile.

'Then none of you wanted to come any more. I know you used to curse us. You did, didn't you?'

Federica nodded again and switched off the smile. She looked up to the top of the mountain. Everything seemed abandoned up there. She could see the stone shelter encircled by vegetation.

'The bar's open, isn't it?' Forte asked the boy.

'Of course it is. It's always open. Open all year round. There's a restaurant too if you want one.'

A gust of wind silenced him. He looked around, stopping on the slope. 'You're going on?' he asked Forte.

'Yes.'

'I'm going back down.'

A moment later he was running and jumping down the slope.

They kept their eyes on him until he disappeared behind a clump of bushes.

'Can you still walk?'

Federica nodded without any change of expression. Once again she stared up at the peak and smiled a strange rapt smile. Forte suddenly thought it might not be a good idea to continue.

'If you want to go back, we can do the climb tomorrow. It's going to rain,' he said, looking at the thick black sky.

Federica started walking upwards again as if she hadn't heard the question.

They walked for another twenty minutes in silence with the sky getting darker and darker. The wind was now stirring up the dust. The path was much steeper and they had to cling on to the rocks and the shrubs.

It seemed to Forte that his daughter had suddenly recuperated all the energy natural to her age: she led the way, with an easy stride; she kept leaving him behind and then pausing to wait, gazing at him with her ironic black eyes. He felt tired.

'It's steeper than I remember or maybe it's just my age,' he puffed, smiling bravely. He pulled himself up with an effort and rubbed his hands on his trousers. Federica set off again at once, granting him no respite.

'Wait . . . what's got into you!' he shouted after her.

Federica was climbing faster than ever. The wind helped her, whereas it drove Forte back and seemed to make all his movements more ponderous.

It started to rain. Irregular, scattered drops carried on the wind. Federica took no notice; she strode on upwards as if she wanted to reach the top as soon as possible.

Forte gave up calling her. He felt worn out. It was a new kind of weariness: his heart was hammering inside his chest; there was a slow ache which irradiated from his left hand to his shoulder and his chest. He tried to pretend it was nothing; he put more energy into his legs. He didn't want her to realise he was having trouble.

The pain in his shoulder increased, then moved down to his stomach, provoking a sense of nausea and dizziness. He slackened his pace, and tried to walk slowly and calmly, in an effort to forget the pain.

'My hand was trembling this morning. Which one?' he asked himself, as if it were someone else's hand he was considering. 'The same one. It could be a heart attack,' he told himself lucidly, continuing to walk.

He glanced up at his daughter: she was climbing with a light swinging movement of her hips and arms; her head remained erect on her shoulders while her pony-tail bounced at each step. For some minutes now she hadn't looked back to see if he were following. She made her way, closed in stubborn solitude.

'She's suffering,' he thought as his pain became unbearable; his eyes glazed over, so that her moving figure became a distant blur.

He closed his eyes. He kept walking for a while without falling. Then he felt the thud of his body against the rocks and the bitter taste of earth pushing its way into his mouth.

'I can't die,' he thought for one instant before abandoning his body to pain. 'Not like this, not now.'

Twenty-One

He could see a figure moving around the room. It was wrapped in a blanket. He couldn't make it out clearly. But it must be a blanket that clothed the figure down to the thighs, leaving the knees, ankles and feet bare.

Slowly, because he felt that each move must be gentle, he raised his eyes: the figure was wandering around; every so often he lost track of it and his eyes roamed in vain search, focusing on empty parts of the strange room.

'Why does it move so quickly?' he thought, giving up his attempts to hold it with his eyes. He shut them.

'Who is it? Where am I?' he wondered with his eyes closed. He opened them again.

The figure walked up and down; he could hear the padding of its bare feet on the floor. Now it halted next to him, and bent over him so closely that his eyes couldn't focus on the face.

He felt the touch of something smooth; he couldn't make out where. He closed his eyes and concentrated on this sensation. He was tired. Under his lowered eyelids he felt his tiredness dissolve in tears, but this time he was too tired to hold them back. That soft touch moved up to his tears, wiped them away, and then broadened out to become a cheek resting against his. He opened his eyes and recognised her.

'What's happened?' he stammered.

Federica's eyes gazed at him in concern; with her hands she signalled that he was not to talk, and then she lifted his hands from where they lay on the sheet and kissed them.

Forte rolled his eyes around the room: the walls were of stone; there was a chair, a table and the bed he was lying on. On the table stood a little light. At ceiling height there was a closed window giving on to darkness.

'It's night. It was daytime when I fell unconscious,' he thought. 'I collapsed on the way up. We're at the top of the mountain then. She must have called someone to carry me up.'

He looked at her again. She hadn't moved. She was caressing his hands with a rapid, light movement. She continued to gaze at him.

'Have I been ill?' he whispered to her.

She nodded. She got up, holding the blanket tight, and moved towards the chair. From one of the anorak pockets she pulled out something that looked to Forte like a notebook. She turned back to him. She settled herself at the end of the bed; as she sat down, Forte caught a glimpse of her naked body.

'Did you get wet?' he asked in a weak voice.

Federica had opened the notebook. Forte recognised her diary. Federica tore a page out, wrote something and placed the paper in front of his eyes.

'You've been ill. You mustn't be afraid. I'm here and tomorrow the doctor will be back. He's already seen you. He says you mustn't move or tire yourself. The owner of the restaurant carried you up.'

'What was the matter?' he asked.

Federica wrote again. Forte read: 'Something to do with the heart perhaps. Tomorrow he'll be able to tell you for certain. You mustn't be afraid. He's given you some sedatives. He says you're strong.'

She looked at him. She was smiling; he smiled back. 'Not all that strong,' he whispered.

Federica wrote again: 'You're sixty. I'm nineteen and I'm already in a bad way.'

Forte smiled wearily. 'You're not ill,' he breathed weakly.

Federica's pen scratched again. Her unbound hair tumbled along her bare arm. The blanket knotted above her breast left her folded legs free.

'She's very beautiful!' thought Forte.

Federica placed a new note before his eyes.

'Don't think too much and keep calm. I know it's difficult. You mustn't be afraid. I'm not. Everything's going to be fine. I could stay with you here for ever. But you're not used to being alone with anyone. After a while you always have to go somewhere else. Whatever you need, I'm here.'

Federica slipped the note into the pages of her diary. She put the diary back in her anorak pocket.

She came back to the bed. Forte had closed his eyes as he saw her returning. He wanted to think about the last sentences of the note, his illness, and what was going to happen.

He felt her settling at the end of the bed; he moved his legs to one side to make room for her; it took a good deal of effort.

'I must be really ill,' he thought, trying to keep calm. 'Tomorrow I'll talk to the doctor. I'll have to go straight back to Rome. How can we stay here in these conditions? Anyway, sooner or later we would have had to go back. She wants to stay on here, but that's because she's not well. How did she realise that I couldn't face it here any longer with her? Now I'll have to call Rome and not say anything to Marta but let Bosio know.'

His heart started to hammer. He feared another attack.

'I mustn't think like this. Now I have to rest. She said so too. But what if you don't know how to? At any rate I mustn't start thinking, or else I'll get worse.'

He breathed deeply to calm the beating of his heart. Amidst his steady sighs, he let out a slight moan. He was afraid she might have heard it. He realised that he was in fact afraid of her closeness, of her body curled up at the end of the bed. He remembered how disturbing he had found the touch of her skin when he woke up.

'But after all, she's like me,' he reassured himself. 'She doesn't like mawkishness. She's dignified in her affections. She's not like the others. She'll get better and she'll be free,' he thought deliriously. 'Free to do whatever she wants to and nobody will be able to make her unhappy. No man. She'll be like me.'

His heart began to make itself felt again in his temples, his arms and his legs. 'I'm going to die. Marta was right. We shouldn't have come here. I wasn't up to it. I've never done anything like this before. I should have left her to Marta, like the others. She's better at this kind of thing. Everybody has his own professional field,' he began to argue, as if he were talking to somebody in the office. 'It's not professional to move into other fields. Only amateurs do that. If it had at least been a son. Again. But there it is.'

He held his breath. He felt his daughter's hand move up the sheet towards his own. He didn't move. He tried to keep as still as possible. He held his breath. Federica's hand was seeking his; now it had found it and started to caress it softly. Forte left his hand lying on the sheet, hoping that she would think he'd gone to sleep. He felt her skin running over his old man's fingers, his slackened skin, his protruding veins. Her hand was light and expert; she was trying to caress him without annoying him. Occasionally she would pause and then start up again.

Forte could no longer feel his heart or anything else. There was just a general fiery throb, and the only cool thing was that light caress at the end of the bed, that touch on his hand. Federica's hand paused, waiting.

Suddenly Forte saw his wife leaning over a cot and pausing in exactly the same way between one caress and another.

Federica's hand slipped slowly from his; her skin moved away with a delicacy calculated not to wake him. He suddenly thought that if her caresses ceased he would die. He gripped her hand and pulled it towards him with all the force he had. Federica slid up the bed next to his body in one rapid movement. Forte felt her clutching his face, covering it with kisses; she kissed him on the forehead, on the cheeks, on the head, she took his hands and kissed them, she hugged and caressed him. But none of these actions seemed separate or distinct; all he was aware of was one long embrace that melted every trace of pain and fear. He opened his eyes and saw her close to his face. She was looking at him with that same serious expression he remembered from when she used to come and play in his study, peering round the door at him, or when he used to go to her room in the evening and she would turn from her desk and gaze at him silently, as if waiting for something.

'I'm not afraid. Are you?' he whispered.

'No . . .' she murmured a moment later.

She lay down next to him and nestled her head on his shoulder. Forte closed his eyes. Only two elusive thoughts flickered through his mind before he fell asleep: he thought that it was very natural to hold his daughter close to him like this and – an instant before sleep enfolded him – that she had spoken.

Twenty-Two

They stayed on the mountain for another three days. The doctor returned the following day and confirmed the heart attack. For the moment he wasn't to move, but as soon as he was better he should go to hospital for a check-up. The Ischian doctor smiled continually as he spoke. He was trying hard to cope with a situation that he would have been very happy to leave to a more experienced colleague. He was cordial and accepted wine from the owner of the restaurant who offered it gladly, happy at this unexpected business out of season.

Forte lay in bed and listened to them discussing his case. He was in a state of torpor and everything seemed to him to be going as it should. He wasn't concerned to know whether he was being looked after properly, whether there was any danger of his dying or what kind of attack he had had. He wasn't interested in such matters. At any other moment in his life, he would have arranged for himself to be taken straight to Rome. But now he saw no need for it.

'They must have heart attacks on Ischia too,' he reasoned, with a touch of complacency as he thought how his Roman friends would have reacted in the same situation. 'They probably don't have so many, but they must happen here occasionally.'

He wasn't bothered about his exact state of health because he was convinced he wasn't going to die. Amidst all his dazed and disconnected thoughts, he felt quite well. Better than he had felt for ages.

The day after, as soon as he woke up to find Federica asleep on his shoulder, his only worry had been his wife. 'She mustn't learn that I'm ill. She mustn't come,' he had thought, looking at his daughter as she slept. 'I'll get over things here, and I'll tell her all about it afterwards.'

He dipped in and out of sleep continually in those days, with never any notion of how long he had been asleep or awake.

He felt as if he remained for ever in the same condition: immersed in a serene limbo made up of thoughts and dreams; of arguments that would be interrupted by memories, which would then turn out to be a movement of his hand or a gesture of his daughter's. But the moment he managed to distinguish a thought from a memory or an action, everything blurred over again, and it seemed to him that it wasn't his daughter who tucked in his blankets for him but some other dream-like presence.

'Illness is something else,' he thought just before dropping off again. 'Dying must be something else. Here there's no need for effort, there's no confusion.

She's here. I must do something for her,' he thought, confusing his daughter's illness with his own. 'What does she keep writing?' he wondered, seeing her at work on her diary in the dim lamplight. 'She's writing her diary.' What had happened to all the ones he'd written? The leather notebook in the jacket of his uniform during the war. The one he'd kept in their first house before any of the children were born; and that other one, when work was going badly and he used to sit in his room at night, smoking on his own.

'I may have got things wrong or right in my life but that's the way it was!' he defended himself against some attacker. 'I did all I could. I never held back.'

He opened his eyes. She was sitting next to him, trying to soothe him. With her cool hands resting on his forehead, she gazed at him searchingly.

'What's the matter?'

'It's nothing,' he stammered. 'I was dreaming. I'm tired.'

She stayed beside him until he fell asleep again. She never left his bedside once during those three nights. She slept curled up at the end of the bed or with her head resting on his shoulder.

Now he was no longer afraid of her proximity.

'What's kept me apart from them all this time?'

He tried to define this new feeling of well-being so as to be able to recall it afterwards. It was an indifference towards his illness, his person, and towards his usual thoughts which now struck him as a pointless mental exercise.

'Where did I go wrong?' he asked himself again,

tightening his arm around his sleeping daughter's shoulders. 'What did I neglect? I've always talked to them about everything. So why should I torment myself? There's no reason for it. I gave them everything. So what do they want from me? What do they want . . . me?' he repeated, tripping over the words. 'They want me,' he suddenly thought. He looked at his hand which trembled slightly on Federica's shoulder. 'Maybe that's what I've never given them. Maybe that's what Marta thinks. But how does one do it? And how is Marta now?' But what came to mind was an image of his wife just after their wedding: she smiled up at him with her girlish face. 'One must see things detachedly, or else go mad.' He looked at his daughter as she slept. 'She's not a child any more. It's not right.'

He delicately removed his arm from her shoulder. 'They turned me into what I am. They want me to die. That's what she wants too.'

Once again he saw his daughter springing lightly up the mountain while he hobbled after her. His heart hammered again inside his chest.

'And so I'm going to die. This is the conclusion.'

He closed his eyes; he could feel the tremor in his left hand increasing. His daughter's body was like an unbearable burden pressing up against him. He tried vainly to shift her.

'What on earth made me give in to her? I've always succeeded in doing what I wanted. Why did I give in to her so quickly? She wants me to die. That's what she wants.'

He realised Federica was getting up from the bed. He opened his eyes.

'I feel bad,' he stammered. 'I feel like I did before.'

She leaned over him. 'I'll get your medicine,' she whispered. 'I'll give it to you at once. Don't worry.'

He followed her with his eyes as she took something from the table and came back to the bed. She picked up the glass of water from the bedside table, pulled him up gently, put a tablet in his mouth and made him drink. She settled his head back delicately on the pillow.

'Tomorrow we'll go home.' She squeezed his hand. 'You'll get better, you'll see.'

'She loves me,' he thought, closing his eyes. 'I've misunderstood everything.'

Twenty-Three

Forte sat in the garden in one of the wicker armchairs. The day was spring-like. A few wispy clouds swept briskly across the sky, which had been washed clean by the last rain.

With his head resting against the back of the chair, Forte followed the movement of the clouds. Every so often he dropped his eyes to the plants in the garden. He remembered, as if it were a remote event, his conversation with Nicoló, the gardener: the son's hostile gaze as his father so imperturbably wrenched the weeds from the beds.

Adele appeared at the french window into the garden.

'Wouldn't you like to come in? Aren't you cold?' she asked.

'I'm fine. What's Federica doing?'

'She's in her room, writing,' she answered, wiping over the marble table between the chairs. 'Shall I call her?'

'Yes, please, ask her to come here a second.'

Forte kept his eyes on her as she dragged her fat body up the stairs.

They had been back a week. Forte had refused to go to hospital; he decided to recuperate at home, with the doctor and a nurse calling each day. It had all turned out as he had wished: his wife and daughters had been told nothing; maybe only his wife had suspected anything.

'You sound strange. Are there any changes?'

He had at once switched the subject to his daughter.

'Yes: Federica is better.' And he had passed her over to her.

His wife couldn't believe it. It seemed like a miracle to her. She was happy — and a little put out because the miracle had been effected by him.

'How did it happen?' she kept asking him on the phone.

Forte didn't know. He was confused. He no longer felt as he had done during those days on the mountain. He didn't know what had happened between them, what had got Federica talking. Had it been his illness or the way they had been thrown together? But anyway, if she was cured, maybe they could think about going back home. At the office nobody had heard about his heart attack. So, for this reason too, it was a good thing it had happened here.

'How do you feel?' She was standing at the french window.

'Fine. Much better. I'm still playing the invalid but I'm really fine. Sit down a moment, won't you?'

She was once again wearing tight jeans; for months she'd given them up in favour of loose-fitting invalid tunics. She had put on just a little weight, and there was more colour in her cheeks.

'Yes, maybe she's cured,' he thought.

'How many pills have they given you today?' she asked in her wavering old-woman's voice. When she spoke her lips always seemed to go dry.

'Three. And you?'

'I just take one a day now,' she said, laughing.

'That was what you wanted, wasn't it?' he laughed too.

They fell silent. This allusion touched something in both of them.

'I wanted to talk to you. Since my attack we haven't talked. I still feel confused. Maybe it's the sedatives.'

He tried to smile. She looked serious, waiting.

'I thought I was going to die. I mean, it wasn't the first time I'd thought such a thing. But for those few days it was a real possibility rather than just a thought. You know, it's strange that I should have fallen ill at the same time as you. But perhaps that's not the point – I'm not being very clear, sorry.'

He glanced at her and thought that perhaps her silence was intended to make him blush. He remembered doing the same thing at the office with his employees.

'I don't know why I'm telling you these things. These last few days I've been thinking about myself, about us, about what happened to us. You know, I always thought I was close to you all . . . to you in particular.'

His thoughts were eluding him, inexpressible. It

was painful for him to present himself like this. He didn't like changes of mind.

'I don't know how to talk about it now.'

'It doesn't matter,' she interrupted him.

'What?'

'How you talk about it.'

'Of course it doesn't,' he said hastily. 'I thought I was close to you all, but it wasn't true. I was taken up with so many other things. But you – while we were up the mountain – you were so close to me,' he said at last, making an effort. 'I never thought such a thing was possible between a father and a daughter. But maybe it had never happened to me with any one.'

As he talked he listened to himself incredulously. How could he be so ingenuous?

'And now all I want is for you to get well, for you to be happy.'

Now I've really gone too far, he thought as he spoke.

'It doesn't mean anything, I know. I imagine all parents wish the same thing, more or less. But not me. I never thought it was important. In fact I've often thought that being happy wasn't particularly intelligent. The fact is that everything happens up here only' – he tapped the tips of his fingers against his forehead. He looked up at her. 'But I always thought that it wouldn't be the same with you and your sisters as with other people, that I would talk to you all and explain to you the way I was. I didn't want to remain silent with you too. That system works perfectly well at work but not with one's children. However, when Silvia grew up and then Caterina and then you, I couldn't stop what was happening inside here' – again he raised his hand to his forehead. 'Well, now it goes on by itself. There's no way of stopping it now. Silvia and Caterina would occasionally ask me about some topic they really cared about. And all I ever wanted was to say nothing, to make them speak their minds. I would watch them and listen to them like some external observer. I studied them, just as I did everybody else. Sometimes I would say to myself: they're your own daughters, you should talk to them, you should find a way to get through to them. But in the end I would always say nothing. And when I saw that this saddened them, I used to get angry because they were incapable of standing up to me. Federica, that's the way I am. I can reason, I can think, but that's it. I can't understand you and your problems, just as I've never been able to understand your sisters.' He lowered his eyes. 'Nor your mother properly, for that matter. Forgive me for spilling all these things out to you in this way, but I'm not used to talking about them.'

'It doesn't matter how you talk about them,' she said again brusquely.

'No, of course it doesn't matter.' He realised his eyes were misting over. He swallowed saliva and clenched his fists like a child. 'It's just that I really can't find the words. I feel tired.' He looked at her.

'How hard she is,' he thought. 'Yes – like me.'

'I love you,' he finally managed to gasp out, as if they were words from another language.

Federica gazed at him without speaking. To Forte it seemed as if she were thinking of something else.

'Caterina once said something like that about you,' she said at last, looking away from her father's face to some remote spot in the garden.

'Really? And what do you think?' he said. 'Have you ever felt happy?'

Federica burst out laughing like a child. 'When someone laughs, it means they're happy,' she then said with a grave expression.

'Don't you want to talk about it seriously?' he asked, irritated by her laughter and her ironic tone.

'How can you talk seriously about happiness? You can't. But maybe there's no real way of talking about it.'

Forte fell silent. He realised that his daughter's words expressed a succinct truth, one of those truths he was always trotting out so glibly.

'When a person like me starts talking about feelings and sentiments, he just gets sentimental,' he thought.

'What do you write in your diary all day?'

'I try to remember things I've forgotten. You know, since I've been like this,' she said in a sad voice.

Forte felt a pang in his heart. He remembered the touch of her hands on his face, the way she had lain curled up next to him. He felt angry at having only talked about himself.

'What have you forgotten?' he asked gently.

'Marco,' she said after a moment's hesitation. She pronounced the name with extreme delicacy, as if she were afraid to spoil it by uttering it. 'I've never spoken to you about him. I've never spoken to anyone about him.'

'Who is he? Someone you studied with?'

'No. I didn't study with him.' She lowered her eyes, fiddling with her hands. 'I . . . we were together.'

Forte felt another pang at his heart, more painful than the previous one. 'You were together?' he stammered. 'Why didn't you ever say anything to us?'

'He wasn't like us. He worked, he didn't study.'

Her chest heaved as she let out a moan. She hid her face in her hands. 'I don't know where he is. He's disappeared,' she sobbed, unable to stop. 'I don't know anything about him. Nobody knows anything.'

Forte stared at her incredulously while she continued to sob.

'Don't cry,' he said after a moment's silence.

Federica hastily dried her face without looking at him.

'How can he have disappeared? And what do you mean, you were together but you don't know anything about him?'

'I know something, but the place where we used to meet, nobody there knows anything about him. I went there but . . .'

'Where?' he interrupted her.

'In a *pensione* near the station.'

Forte had the feeling that the chair was beginning to tremble beneath him. The garden wall, the plants and the window all flickered indistinctly before his eyes.

'A *pensione* near the station. Why?'

'That was where he lived. But now they all say he didn't, he never stayed there at all.'

Forte tried to collect his thoughts. 'But who was he? Where did you meet him? What was he doing at the station? You never told us anything – why not?'

Federica fell silent.

'You must explain, how can I understand otherwise?' he said, trying to keep calm.

Federica gazed at him for a moment without answering. 'I don't know his surname. I don't know what he did at the station. I just know he worked in a bar. He did other jobs but I don't know what they were.'

'But why did you keep him from us?'

'I never talked about him because there was no reason to.'

'What do you mean, no reason?' he shouted. 'Why was there no reason?'

'When I wrote his name, you didn't believe it.'

'What does that mean? I thought he was a friend of yours, a university friend. And am I supposed to believe you now?' His voice was getting louder again, as his temper ran away with him. 'You can't even remember his surname! You don't know where he is! You used to meet in a *pensione* near the station, do you really expect me to believe all this?'

'He never told me his surname,' she said with an effort, lowering her eyes.

'How could that be? You went out together and you don't know a thing about him. Why did you meet at the station? Didn't he have a home?'

'I don't know. Maybe he wasn't from Rome. He sometimes talked about a place where he was born.'

'Listen to me,' said Forte, moving his hands towards hers without touching them. 'I'm trying to understand. It's not easy, I never imagined you led this kind of life. How did you meet?'

'At the university. He used to go and hang around there when he wasn't working.'

'And what did you do? Make a kind of pact that you wouldn't tell each other anything?'

'No. When we met, he said he could see I was a posh sort of person, someone who studied, he meant. But he didn't care about things like that, he just wanted to spend a few hours a day with me just to . . . to make love,' she mumbled, without looking at him. 'Maybe he did it with other girls too.'

Forte stared at her, unable to take it in. 'And that was all right with you?' he managed to say at last.

'Yes, it was all right. He didn't want to tell me what he did, but neither did I.'

'Why?'

'Just didn't. He didn't know anything about my life, my exams, the university. He only passed that way because he liked the square.'

'And why didn't you say anything to us?'

'Because you don't know these things.'

'What?'

Federica wrung her hands. 'The station and the rest of it.'

'The rest of what?'

190

Federica didn't reply. Forte felt that he was about to lose his patience.

'What sort of people do you find at the station? Pretty unhappy types, I should think, without jobs, without homes, drop-outs.'

Federica was looking at him now, flushed and strangely exalted. 'I was one of them!' she suddenly shouted. 'I was there too! You know nothing! You don't know about my life, you don't understand a thing!'

'Well, explain yourself then,' he said coldly.

'No, you wouldn't understand!' she said, trembling in every part of her body. She stood up.

'Sit down, don't behave like this!'

'No,' she muttered, her eyes full of tears. 'You're too wicked to understand.'

Federica turned quickly and ran indoors.

'Federica!' he called, getting to his feet. 'Come here!'

She ran upstairs and disappeared behind a slammed and locked door.

Forte dropped back into his armchair. 'I'm too tired,' he mumbled to himself. 'I must rest. I'll go and see her later.'

He stared at his hands which lay inert on the arms of the chair.

'Pandemonium has come upon us. Utter confusion. We should have been stricter with her earlier. Perhaps he was right,' he thought, recalling what his son-in-law had said and how he had disparaged it. 'I went about everything the wrong way with her.'

He rested his head back in the chair and looked up at the sky. Black clouds were gathering again.

'It's cold now; you must go in again. Otherwise I'll phone your wife and tell her everything.' Adele had come up to the chair. She was staring at him, aware of what had happened; her hands were on her hips, and her expression was disapproving.

She helped him to stand up even though he told her he felt fine. He heard her murmur something as she pulled the window to.

'What did you say?' he asked her sharply, as he settled in the armchair by the fire.

'She's a good girl,' she said with an offended air.

'Of course she is. Who ever said she wasn't?'

She was bustling around him, waiting for a chance to talk. He pretended not to see her.

'Shall I call her?' she said, moving towards the kitchen.

'No. Leave her alone. Later.'

'Good boys, good girls,' thought Forte. 'They're all good boys and girls. What did she go to the station for? This time I'll force her to tell me. They're all liars. But this time she'll talk. Yes, later, when she's calmed down, she'll talk.'

He paused to reflect on a way of getting her to talk, a way of tackling the matter. Then he went on to think about the office and all the work he'd left there, about Bosio and how he should have phoned him to tell him not to come just yet. He decided to call him. He spent an hour on the phone, taking decisions, asking him about documents and getting him to read them out.

After the phone-call he felt in good shape. All this

attention to business matters had made his mind keener and sharper: he felt ready to face his daughter.

He felt sure that everything could be cleared up by a long and intimate chat with her after dinner. She was cured now, after all.

When it was time for dinner he knocked at her door to tell her that everything was ready. Adele had gone off; she had left the table set and the meal prepared.

'I don't want to eat,' she answered without opening the door.

'Even if you don't want to eat, I'd like to talk to you. Come down to the living-room, I'll be waiting for you.'

'I'm not coming. I want to be alone.'

Her voice behind the door was determined and there seemed to be a note of challenge in it as well.

'Open up! I can't stand out here talking to you like this.'

There was a long silence. Then he heard her bare feet on the floor. They approached the door. As a child she had always walked around barefoot. The key turned slowly in the lock; the door opened a mere slit, revealing her pale face.

'I don't want to keep you waiting. I'm writing you a letter, but it'll take time. Here, have this,' she said at last, slipping a notebook through the crack. 'Read it. I don't care how much of it you understand, all I'm interested in is finding Marco. Read it all, but especially the last few pages.'

Forte took the notebook. She closed the door at once.

It was a school exercise-book. Forte opened it, and in the semi-darkness of the corridor read the title and the opening sentences: 'Diary of Federica Forte, begun 1 November 1982.'

He shut it again, looked at the door, and went down the stairs. He sat in the armchair; he stared at the table set for dinner, at the cover of the notebook, and then began to read.

Twenty-Four

First of all I should organise things and decide just how I intend to keep this diary. It isn't going to be a typical diary, like those written by young ladies in the nineteenth century who merely recounted their disappointments in love and then wrote nothing else after their marriage. I'm not interested in that kind of thing. Nor will it be a diary that relates the events of the day because they're mostly not very interesting. I'm writing this diary to remember and to put my thoughts in order.

When people talk, it's never about the distant past and maybe not even the recent past. These things are generally to be found in books. Since I wouldn't know how to write one for other people's use, I've decided to keep a diary.

The form: I'll try to write without continually correcting myself; since it's only for myself, if a sentence doesn't turn out right, I'll leave it as I wrote it. Essays at the university have to be written the way the professors write, but here

I want to write my own way. I know all the objections: everything you write should be done well, there's a correspondence between the form and the contents, the study of language etc., etc. . . . at the end of the year I'll be taking the exam in philosophy of language and maybe this will be my last chance to write just the way I feel.

The lay-out: the diary will be divided into three parts.

The first could be called my story or my life or just me, and it'll contain everything that concerns me directly, not in chronological order.

The second part will consist of observations on what I'm studying. It's a well-known fact that no university student manages to produce his or her own observations. It's not so well known that they could in fact write whole volumes; personally I've picked up so many philosophical ideas among my friends that I'm sure that if we got together we could write a new text-book. I'll confine myself to recording my own, although I'll make occasional use of quotations from authors who have said similar things to me.

The third part will deal with other people as I see them. I'll record their behaviour, sometimes just by noting down some odd sentence.

If one of these parts takes off while another stays put, it won't matter. Psychologists who study the 'age of development' (I found it in the encyclopaedia one day when my friends and I were trying to define ourselves) could spin all sorts of theories from it. Luckily it'll never get into their hands.

If I have any other methodological notes to write, I'll add them here later.

These methodological notes, as she termed them, were followed by some sentences which had been added only recently.

Ischia, February 1984: now I only ever write in the first part of this diary. All the rest has come to a halt. Ever since Marco disappeared it's all had no meaning. I'm trying to remember and to write down the few things I knew about him, and which have come to mind for the first time now; in this way I'm trying to work out what could have made him disappear like that. There's still a good deal of confusion in my mind. I can't remember why or when I tore out the pages in which I'd written about him. I don't understand what can have happened on that day – whenever it was – when I saw a sudden strange flame sweep before my eyes. And after that, nothing. When I went back to this diary, I realised that just before I fell ill the first two parts had come to a halt. I couldn't write anything about myself or about the things I was studying. Even now I can't. For me, writing means looking for Marco. I wrote something about my father when we arrived. I thought he had brought me here to help me. But he can't get out of himself. He isn't capable of it. Now I realise that in her own way Mamma has always loved me more than he does. But I always went running after my father more than anyone else. I was close to him when he was ill. He was adrift and no longer in control of everything. I was happy to look after him. When he was asleep I kissed his hands. That skin of his, which I had never been able to touch, made me feel good. While we were up Mount Epomeo I thought that everything would be different between us afterwards, that he would still look at me in that same gentle way when he woke up each morning and the intimacy between us would last for ever like a pact. We would never deny it out of fear of being weak. But things haven't turned out that way. Now he's resumed that businesslike detached tone of his; he talks about himself and he still tries to put me down. He's defending himself. As usual, I started to defend myself too. Then I gave up. I've felt different ever since his illness. I've no desire to play that game any more. I never stop thinking about Marco.

A few blank pages followed. Forte turned them slowly, in time to the beating of his heart. His eyes were clouding over; the lines of neat, childish handwriting on which his future seemed to depend blurred into one another. He had never read anything that had hit him so hard. He let his eyes flicker over the page for a moment, then started reading again.

My story, my life. 1 November 1982
 Today I enrolled in the philosophy faculty. I'm not exactly sure why. I supposed that there one might get to talk about things that otherwise never get talked about at all. I felt awful. The university is an immense place full of strange people. I felt overwhelmingly nostalgic for school. I don't know anything about them. I don't want to know anything. I phoned Carlo and Giulia. They couldn't understand things either and felt bewildered.

5 November
 I've got nothing to do. I went and stood outside the school gates. I reflected on the fact that every other year, on November 5th, I was there. I had already bought all the set books and notebooks. I used to wrap them in cellophane and sniff them because I love the smell of stationery. Everybody was in class and it was all quiet. Saverio was in the caretaker's lodge and when he saw me he invited me in. He was pleased to hear I'd enrolled at the university. He says I'm the right sort. But I was pleased to be there with him. From the kitchen I could smell cabbage. His wife made a fuss over me too. She came out of the kitchen in a dirty apron and kissed me. I stayed there and chatted with them, sitting in their rickety old red armchair. I've sat

there so many times when I've been ill, waiting for Mamma to come and fetch me. When Saverio got up to ring the bell I left so as not to see them all come out.

8 November

I'm nobody. Papà believes I'm one thing. Mamma another. My sisters never have any time, now that they're married. Only I know that I'm not anything yet. I don't know how you become something. By going to school, to university, living in a family, travelling. 'I think, therefore I am,' says Descartes. If you think, you're someone. But thoughts can go along by themselves as well. Nowadays we're used to thinking. We've done it for centuries. I try and work out if there's ever been a moment when I was someone. Maybe only when they registered my birth. I got my birth certificate for the university. There everything's very clear. Maybe I'll be someone on my death certificate as well. I wonder who'll do it. My children maybe, if I have any. I'll have registered their births and they'll do my death. Perhaps it's the registry office that knows everything. I'm only ever anyone in my room; there everything is clear and orderly. But the more orderly I make things in my room, the more unbearable it gets to leave it. Maybe I shouldn't leave it at all.

30 November

I'd like to know what other people think. I

reckon I might manage to love them if I only had some idea. The only thing of any importance is what you think using your own head. That's what my father says.

2 December

It's cold. I'd like to live under a light blanket which would shelter me from the outside world. Under the blanket I could keep my smells and I'd always know that I existed as well. I've bought a light Peruvian shawl. I wrap myself in it when I come back from the university. Sometimes I feel my arms and legs escaping. Everything has a life of its own. I feel I have so many questions to ask that if I started I'd have to shut up. Now I always follow the same route to the university. I buy peanuts at the corner by the hospital and I always sit at the same desk in the front row. I know that nobody will sit next to me. It's too close to the professor. Carlo, Giulia, Miriam and Fabio have disappeared. We never meet up any more.

14 December

I've got one bond with my body and another with my thoughts. I play with them. I make them work when I need them. I never have the feeling that I'm a whole person. Everything is a game inside your head. You just have to learn it and play it as required. Every so often they change the rules, but then all you need do is follow the new ones and if you do it well enough nobody will realise that you don't know what the aim is. You have to be very adaptable. I feel good on my own.

20 December
I'm cold.

2 January
I've been ill. I had a temperature and to tell the truth I felt good in bed. I kept sleeping and waking up. When I was small my grandmother used to sit on the side of the bed and read to me. I've always thought of illness as a place of fairy-tales and dreams. I used to fall asleep while she was reading and it was fun to wake up and find her still reading. It was like a story that never ended and I felt I knew the bit I hadn't heard just as well as the rest of it. My favourite book as a child was 'Moby Dick'. I loved the descriptions of the whales and all the work they did when they'd caught them. I love detailed descriptions; they're so real.

10 January 1983
I saw Giulia again. We spent the whole afternoon together at her house. There was nobody there. There's never anybody at her house. We didn't talk about the university. She's doing economics and business studies but she didn't want to discuss them. We embraced on the sofa. She doesn't like boys. She's only ever had affairs with girls. I've known for ages that I was the

one she really fancied; but I truly don't love women in that way. I don't even like my own body so I'm certainly not interested in seeing another one just like it. She petted me. I let her because I didn't want to hurt her. She murmured all these sweet nothings. I think she must have read them in some teenage romance. It was really quite sweet. I closed my eyes so as not to laugh. She was really funny. Then she whispered into my ear that I was 'the woman she's always dreamed of', and I burst out laughing. She started to cry and I consoled her. She was so scrawny that I felt quite tender towards her. It struck me that with us both feeling as desperate as we were then, we could have started up again. But it was all over for Giulia. I don't know why people have to work themselves up in that fashion just so as to establish a relationship with someone else. For me the most erotic feeling is tenderness. To tell the truth sometimes I realise that there can be a bit of violence mixed up in it too, but that's only because the other person seems so remote from you that you'd like to pull him towards you. As for all the other perversions that you see in films or you read about, I don't understand them; nor the words they use to talk about them.

6 February

Yesterday I reflected on my life. There's nothing special about it. It's no different from so many other people's. I was born in 1964 (register office); I'm the youngest daughter of a well-off married couple; my father spends his life at the office; my mother lives at home, and she tries (especially now that we're grown up) to spend as much time with us as possible; I've got two other sisters. I was at home for three years; then I went to nursery-school, then high school, then university. My two sisters didn't finish their university studies because they got married. I'm racking my brains to find something else to say. All I can see in front of me is my father's face. He must know something else about me. Not my mother. She sees me as a part of herself. And so she can't know anything about me. Maybe my father doesn't either because he's not a part of anybody. All my mother knows about is when she was expecting me, when she gave birth to me and breast-fed me; when I walked along holding her hand. Whenever I have a problem she immediately thinks it's because of something that she did or didn't do. I'm one of my mother's ribs. My father's washed his hands of me. He goes out every morning and mixes with other people and knows what has to be done; he must have had some plans for me. When I was born he leaned over the cot to get to know me. My mother kept me by her bed and didn't bother looking at me because she knew me already. And when my father first saw me he must have thought: I'll teach you first this then that, and then you'll be able to go out every morning like me and mix with other people. I was asleep in the cot but I could hear him all the same. That's how it must have been. No, I don't think so.

Forte stopped reading. His eyes came to rest on the table set for two. It was like a table with plaster food. He thought of the meals they had all eaten together on that table. As he ran his eyes over the furniture in the room, over the coloured tiles on the floor, the staircase with its wrought-iron handrail, the paintings of seascapes, the books heaped on the shelves, he thought how all those tattered, battered objects now seemed to be summed up in that cold lunch laid for two. All the actions of his life – his life at work and his life in the family – flickered before him in a speeded-up sequence: he saw all his awakenings, all his arrivals at work and arrivals on holiday, his departures and eagerly awaited return journeys. All those things he had steadily and suc-cessively created – his daughters, his house, his work, the garden, the growth of every single thing he'd given life to – seemed to be summed up in the diary he held in his hands.

His mind went back to the arguments that had embittered the weeks before their departure for Ischia. All of them trying to assert their own theories by destroying everybody else's. His daughters and his wife all at it – and his own stubborn attempt to go on reasoning in his usual way without getting anywhere.

Their euphoric departure and then the endless evenings of silence. His perpetual grappling with inadequate and contradictory explanations and theories. Finally his illness and that intimacy they had achieved on the mountain. She had helped him just by staying by his side. There they had been the same thing. But it had only lasted those few days. That was what she had said in her diary. It was the truth.

'Inside your own head you can think anything. "A game inside your head," as she puts it. There's a limit to thoughts and there's a limit to all the freedom I've enjoyed. I never believed that my life could influence anybody. It was all inside my head. And I wanted her life to be like mine. I imagined she would be strong. She was weak and lonely and became more so. Like me.'

He felt as if this last thought had detached itself from him and was wandering freely around the objects in the room. He immediately felt an extraordinary sense of restfulness.

The room with all its imperfections, the clutter that had accumulated over the years, the odd collection of abandoned books and, beyond these, the garden with all its plants that had grown and died, and the whole island: it all seemed to him like a kingdom he had always had in mind, he had always pondered on, but had never actually lived in.

He returned to the diary, with the sensation that it was Federica, his daughter, who was talking to him at that moment: he imagined he could see her in front of him, winding her long hair round her fingers as she talked, fiddling with it when she had something particularly difficult to say, and breaking off every so often to ask him what he thought.

20 January

I'm under the blankets with the window open. There's a slight smell of grass from outside. God knows where from. I feel like crying. It was all going so well. I didn't feel awful any more. I was managing really well. And now everything's confused again. I should close the window to stop the smell of grass getting in and making me cry. But I can't get up. I'm sure that if I don't stay under the blankets the cold will make me feel even worse.

2 February

My exams are in a month's time. I know they'll go well. The epistemology professor always asks me to speak in the seminars. He said I have my own style and ideas. Actually all I do is repeat his ideas in another form. He's never realised.

14 February

I'd like to find someone to be close to.

10 March

I took the exam, full marks. Now I'm waiting to tell Papà when he comes home. I feel as if I don't know any of the things I studied any more. A boy who was waiting to take the exam with me said that's always the way. But I think

I'll never know anything again. Mamma left a bunch of anemones on my desk for me. It's wrong of me to be so concerned with Papà. Mamma deserves it far more.

21 April

I spend whole days of sheer horror, shut up in my room, thinking. It's strange that nobody realises. Mamma gets on with her own things; Papà goes off to work. I hate his work. He must love it more than all of us. He must love his room, his desk, the people he's in charge of, just as I love my room. Each of us lives in our own little closed circle. I don't know who I'm like. I don't even know who I would like to be like. My father, perhaps, because he manages best of all of us. But he's incapable of any simple gesture. That's the only kind of gesture my mother's capable of. There's something terrifying in my mother's words. Like my sisters' now that they're married. I'll do all I can not to be like them.

27 April

Last night I dreamt that Papà died amidst general indifference. Nobody went to see him. Everybody just gave me crazy answers: it's a good thing he's dead because he was mean, a good thing because he hated everybody. I was choked with grief and I couldn't answer any point they made. Then I went to see him: he was drained of colour but he was still moving; he tried to ask me something in a low voice but I couldn't hear him. I woke up with a start, and I still felt frightened, even though I was awake.

8 May

I realise that everything has changed since I left school and started university. When I was at school I thought that what we did there would go on afterwards. But they were children's games. As soon as you go into the world outside you can't breathe by yourself. I don't understand anything. I'm not familiar with my own self. Know yourself and you still know nothing. And yet my father who never listens to anyone but himself has succeeded in beating everybody. Why can't I? I miss other people. Why doesn't he? He's strong, he can do without them. I squeeze my breasts with my hands. I wish I didn't have them. I'd like to cut them off. Maybe it's because I feel this way that I'm not strong like him. There's a touch of spring in the air. Rome is beautiful at this time of year. After lectures I always sit on the wall outside the faculty building for a while. I like the fresh air. The sky's that same blue you find in children's drawings.

There followed a blank page and then several pages had been torn out; there was just a cluster of ragged fragments clinging to the staples. The diary began again after this gap. The handwriting was now uncertain and tremulous, like an old woman's.

Ischia, February

I don't know what day it is. I can hardly see anything. I'm in the bedroom at the top of Epomeo. Papà has had a heart-attack, now he's asleep. There's just a little light on next to the bed. He'll get over it, I'm sure. I secretly hugged him while he was asleep. I hold his hand and he squeezes it without realising. It's a narrow bed but I slept beside him. He opened his eyes twice during the night and looked at me without saying anything, as if he couldn't see me. I touched his face which still had earth on it and his bare arms. He's very calm when he's asleep. I put my feet between his and they were cold.

Three days have gone by. The doctor has come. Papà is better. I've eaten today. My throat hurts less than it used to. I realised that Papà was watching me while I ate and he smiled at me. He can't eat anything. We're both better.

Tomorrow we're going back home. Now and then I exchange a few words with Papà, but most of the time he sleeps and when he wakes up he seems lost in his thoughts. Now I'm the one who wishes he would talk a bit more. He's afraid of me when I get too close to him. This afternoon he woke up while I was resting beside him and I realised that he felt awkward with me so close. I moved to the end of the bed so as not to bother him. When I was ill I didn't want people to get too close either.

Tonight Papà pulled me towards him. I'm

writing in the very first light of dawn. From the window of this room I can see the outlines of the island and the sea gradually coming into focus. I couldn't sleep any longer. I kept thinking of his hand pulling me towards him. My heart was beating. I was just falling asleep and he pulled me towards his face. We held each other close without feeling ashamed. I could feel him trembling a little, but then he calmed down.

We're back home. Papà spends all the time in an armchair. He hasn't said anything to Mamma. Everything's changed between us. Just as it used to be. I eat even though I'm not hungry. I want to go back to Rome and look for Marco. Papà talks to me about little details, as usual. Once again nothing touches him. I ask myself whether what happened up the mountain was real or not. Papà says he's understood a lot of things since we've been here. Good for him. I can't understand the one thing I care about: what's happened to Marco. I can't ever bring this subject up. He won't give me an opening. I'm afraid of it. I try to recall those days – however many they were – when we met at the *pensione*. It's suddenly struck me that I should have gone to Sandro's parents' shop to ask them. Why didn't I think of it? Other things are coming to mind as well, bit by bit.

Something must have happened around the time when I was taking the philosophy of language exam. I was studying with Sandro. He had started up again without telling Marco. I think he was doing it because he wanted to be with me rather than for the exam's sake. He told me that if he started studying again, he'd prefer something practical. I think he meant something like information technology. I remember that we talked about it in the bar after the lecture. I convinced him that philosophy of language was better. Information technology would be out of fashion in a month or two anyway and then they'd think up something else. He came round to my way of thinking and said that it was more original as well. We were studying that book by Saussure. Sometimes on a bench, sometimes at the bar. We didn't know where to go. We were worried that Marco might find out that he'd started studying again. He wouldn't understand. He used to say that the kind of specialisation you need for a job can't be had at a university.

I could never make out what his job was. He never talked to me about it. But when he asked about Sandro and the exam, and I realised that he'd guessed everything, I thought he felt left out. He became rough towards me at the end. I don't know why. I know nothing about his family or his life in general. I can remember every tiny detail of his body. He was so gentle when we made love. I've never met such a gentle person as he was. But he was only like that when we were in bed together. He never told me anything. Just once he laughed and said that he was born in a necropolis, so they didn't miss him much back home. He actually used the word necropolis; it was odd because he never used complicated words. He didn't know any. But now I remember that he knew strange things about churches. Once we passed the church in piazza Esedra. We were waiting for Sandro and he didn't come so we decided to go in. We walked around inside. Marco didn't know anything about the church's date. I didn't know much either, but I realised that it must be baroque or thereabouts. In a family like mine you know these things instinctively. But clearly not in his. Anyway at a certain point he said: 'It's strange; the transept in this basilica is wider than the nave. Let's go and look at the apse.' Something like that. He suddenly sounded like a book. So I asked him how he happened to know about churches. He laughed and didn't explain. That was the only time I ever heard him talk about something different from the usual topics. I guessed he must have read those things in a guidebook somewhere. He really liked directions, schedules, rules.

While we were in the church he decided to listen to a description of it recorded on one of those phone-machines. We listened to it together. I can remember that moment clearly because his face was so different from the way it usually looked. Obviously he was thinking about something I know nothing about. I was paying very little attention to the recording but I remember that at a certain point I started to listen to it more closely. I've always liked the curious little facts they tell you about places. For instance about someone being beheaded there or seeing bones in the catacombs. It gives me the idea that the spirit of those people is still there. Just before the recording finished, the voice told the story of a statue in the church. I can't remember the name of the sculptor, just that he was French and the statue was of a Carthusian monk and was so well made that a famous visitor once said that the only reason it couldn't speak was that it was against the rules of the Carthusians. I remember thinking that it wasn't a bad rule. It often came to mind afterwards. I always thought of Marco's face together with the statue of the Carthusian. When Marco disappeared, for days on end – I don't know how many – I kept going back to the *pensione* to look for him. They lied, pretending they'd never heard of him. Nobody knew anything. I waited whole mornings in front of the faculty building. I used to come home and no one there knew about him. I started to get my memories mixed up. Nobody could help me sort things out in my head. I can't remember why we stopped seeing one another or how long afterwards it was when I started looking for him.

I remember being ill. But when? I don't remember ever tearing the pages out of the diary. And yet that's the only proof I have that something happened. I remember how memories flickered out of my head. I remember feeling scared at night before falling asleep: scared at the thought of waking up and having to go on with my search. Scared that maybe I'd made everything up. I've always made things up. I can make anything up and claim that that's the way things are. I tried to stop thinking about it all. I started studying again and writing about things that didn't involve me. But everything seemed unreal and the only certain memory I had was the feeling of Marco's body lying next to me on the bed in the *pensione*. Then I realised that as I tried to live like other people, not thinking about these things, I was gradually losing my memories and thus the only thing that gave me any joy at all was slipping from my mind. I stopped talking without even realising I was doing so.

Papà didn't believe what I told him. There's no trace of Marco in our life, so he could be right. Maybe I did make everything up. I was on my own, it was a spring day, and one's imagination and sense of loneliness can get stirred by the spring. In the university square I saw a boy walking by and I remembered he'd asked me for a cigarette a month before. He was short and thin but carried himself as if he were all muscles. His hair was fairly long, over his shoulders, and maybe not particularly clean. I went up to him. I felt like stopping him. You can't always look at people as they pass you. So I used the pretext of the cigarette. He let me have a drag on his and smiled at me with his mouth and eyes. We kissed a few days later. We spent every afternoon together, I don't know how long for. Sometimes just to make love, sometimes for short walks in the area around the station. Sometimes he didn't turn up. And other times I didn't go. Especially if I had an exam coming up. Marco introduced me to Sandro. We all hung around together without knowing much about one another. Later I talked more to Sandro. His life before he met up with Marco was closer to my own. So we talked about things connected with the university. I never talked about these things to Marco. He never learnt anything about my life or my family. It wasn't a pact or even a decision. It just happened that way. As I write about it now, what I'm trying to work out is this: how did we live all those months without telling each other anything? It seemed normal to me. In fact, the only thing that made any sense in the world. Relationships based on love all seemed fake to me. But actually that wasn't the point either. The fact was I couldn't get along with anyone. I was always thinking about other people. I wanted them. But as soon as anyone got close, I found myself appalled by the way they differed from me. I couldn't prevent myself from treating them badly and then when they left me I would miss them. It happened several times. And then it stopped altogether because I made sure I never met anyone.

Before Marco I was alone. Even leaving my room was painful. I could only get by on my own, in my room, among the objects I love. There I liked to think about far-off people in other countries. I imagined that I would get along with them in a wordless harmony. Marco was the only person who never asked me anything or told me anything. I don't know why. He was like me in this. If there was a reason for it, I don't know what it was. It was my strongest link to him. Now it strikes me as terrible that I don't understand anything about those months, that I never knew him. I try hard to think the way I thought then, as if I had to explain it to someone. But I have such a strong desire to understand what happened and to find out where he is, that I can no longer imagine our life as it was then. Occasionally a few feelings return: I used to like the fact that at home nobody knew about him, that I gave them nothing to chew over; I used to enjoy thinking of the bed in the *pensione*, the awful furniture, and our bodies pressed up against one another, while they engaged in one of those discussions in which they all just went on contradicting one another. I felt I was above them all because every afternoon I went to a place where there were no words, no plays on words, no doubts, no cynicism, no malice, no intelligence. Maybe there was nothing. Every now and then I find myself thinking so and it's terrifying. I touch the anklet that Marco gave me and try to remember why we used to go to places and meet people. Everything seems so vague, as if I were looking into a story that had happened to somebody else. And yet at the time I was convinced that our secret set us above them, made us stronger than they were. I remember how I felt, looking into my father's eyes and thinking how disappointed he would be if he were to see me together with Marco. I couldn't talk to him about it, because like the coward I am, I wouldn't have been able to bear his disappointment; even as I spoke to him I would have felt ashamed of Marco and of myself. I didn't want to. By saying nothing I kept my pride. So, when I was with Papà, I could despise Marco and the girl who went out with him; and I could despise Papà and all the others, myself included, when I met Marco at the *pensione* Aurora. I'm nobody. Maybe I'm just wicked and damned. Or maybe even this is melodramatic and excessive. Maybe the only word is nothing. Oh God, help me! Don't make me suffer like this any longer. Let me just find some tiny thing of value like a little medal one can wear all the time or a dried flower left in a book. This is melodramatic and romantic as well. How do these things manage not to be so? Who gives them their strength? Why are we so weak?

'Thou dost preserve the stars from wrong; and the most ancient heavens, through Thee, are fresh and strong.' I know it by heart. I don't remember what it is from. I always repeat it when I feel awful and at once I think of the journey I'm going to make and I feel better. I don't want to write any more. Nothing at all.

There followed strange line-drawings: houses, flowers, trees. All drawn as children draw them.

Forte had gone on reading almost automatically, without even properly understanding the meaning of each word. In his daughter's thoughts he recognised many of his own, as if her life were undergoing that same decline that had set into his life all those years before.

'Blinded by thoughts. Thoughts achieve nothing. Who's Marco?' he asked himself for the first time, turning the pages of the diary.

He looked for some further note on that unknown, missing boy. But that was the end of the diary as a diary. There were a few more pages of philosophical quotations and of comments on the family. Forte read them quickly. The first few pages were ordered and neat. Federica had gathered together a good many quotations, copying them down one after the other without their authors' names. Forte guessed the sources of a few of the more famous ones. He attributed some other sentences in a more familiar tone to his daughter. The quotations were all on the same theme: the concept of goodness for a person without religion.

The sequence of beautifully handwritten quotations was not motivated, as it would have been in his case, by the desire to embellish arguments that the writer didn't really believe in; there was clearly an urgent passion to seek out truth for its own sake. Towards the end of the diary her emotional and intellectual confusion increased visibly: there were half-finished sentences, garbled thoughts, fragments of quotations and drawings. Her illness was so clear in these last few pages that Forte couldn't go on. He felt unbearable pity. He stopped reading, rested his head back in the armchair and closed his eyes.

'You don't have to read all of it.'

Forte opened his eyes and saw her at the top of the staircase. She was sitting on the first stair and had been gazing at him for some time perhaps.

'I didn't hear you. Come down,' he said in a voice that came out hoarsely.

'You don't have to read it all. Towards the end I just wrote stupid things. I . . . I never finished it. It was when I was studying, but there's nothing important,' she said without moving.

'Come here, please,' Forte repeated.

'I didn't give it to you to read so that you could see how I write. I'm not interested in that sort of thing. I'm not interested in fine writing or in being . . . anyway, there's not even anything very intelligent.'

'Please come here.' He couldn't get anything else out. He just wanted her to come to his side. 'We can't talk at this distance.'

'Why not? We've always done so. When have we ever needed to feel close in order to talk?' she asked him hollowly.

'I need to now.'

'So did I earlier, now I don't.'

They fell silent. Forte gazed at the notebook and then closed it. He looked up at her again. She was still sitting there motionless and observing him with hostility. He rose to his feet slowly. They stared at each other without saying a word. Forte approached the stairs.

'A person can't just disappear like that,' he said going towards her. 'You've been ill, that's why you can't remember.'

'I've looked for him everywhere. Everything I know is written there. I can't remember what happened.'

Federica buried her face in her hands. She often did this when she was unable to continue talking.

Forte stood still at the bottom of the stairs. Federica lifted her face, wiped her eyes and stared at him for a moment in silence.

'You mustn't stand there like that,' she said. 'It's bad for you.'

She came down the stairs. They stopped one in front of the other.

Forte lifted his hand uncertainly towards her face. 'Let's go and sit down then,' she said, blocking his hand and holding it between her palms in a quick businesslike gesture. 'You can't stand there like that, you'd better lie down. You're not well yet.'

As his hand dropped, he realised that she had let him read the diary, thus presenting him with the wretched chronicle of her days and of what had happened to her, because she had decided that there could be no reciprocal comprehension between them. The decision to lay open her most intimate thoughts to him had sealed the end of all expectations she might have had of him. It hadn't been an act of love but of resignation. He felt he had lost her.

Twenty-Five

Forte lay on his bed in his room, smoking and looking at his daughter who was sitting opposite him in an armchair by the window.

It was a scene he had often seen between his two elder daughters and his wife. They used to come into the room on summer mornings while his wife was still in bed and he was shaving. They would bring her coffee and then stay there chatting and exchanging confidences – his wife sitting up in bed and her two daughters by her side. Fragments of their conversation and laughter would reach him in the bathroom. Then he would go downstairs for breakfast, leaving them free to talk. Sometimes they came in with strained faces, one of them red-eyed from crying. They would close the door; then he knew that some drama was being enacted and in the evening he would have to remember to ask his wife about it and express concern.

Now it was up to him to play the central role.

'Can't you remember when it happened or at least when you met?' he asked her after a moment's silence.

'There are some things I remember. I took the exam in October. The date's written in my registration book. Nothing had happened at that point. After that I don't know. I can't sort out the different periods of time in my mind. Sometimes I think one thing, and sometimes another. I can't even talk about it,' she said, her voice trembling.

'What was this *pensione* where you used to meet?'

Federica looked at him without answering. She twisted her hair on one side and started to gnaw her fingernails, shifting her eyes from him.

'I only ever went into his room; I don't know about the rest of it. There were a lot of coloured people. Marco knew them. They always said hello to him but he never replied. Maybe because I was with him. There was a woman at the desk. Sometimes it was her, sometimes her husband. They always said hello to Marco. When I went back there, asking after him, she looked at me as if she'd never seen me before. She couldn't remember Marco either.'

'And what about Sandro – did he live in the *pensione* as well?'

'Yes, they slept in the same room. Marco had bought a little stove. They made an exception for him, because you weren't supposed to cook anything in the rooms there. There was a coloured woman with a little baby who used to come to our room . . . his room, to heat up her bottle. She was the only person I ever got to know. She was from Somalia. She was looking for a job with a family, but she couldn't find anything because of the baby. She couldn't leave him at a school or anything, because he was too small. The baby wasn't well, he was always crying. Marco tried to help her, he gave her some money. She told me about her husband who had gone back to Somalia with the elder son because it's not easy for men to get jobs with families. After he left, her milk dried up. She was always thinking about the money she was going to send him from here. She was very young.'

Federica looked up at her father.

'For a while she found a job in the afternoon and left the baby with us. We used to take him to the university square to get some fresh air. Sometimes when Marco came to pick me up he brought the baby along. Then she left. She'd decided to try another city. Turin I think. We never saw her again. She wasn't with us for very long.'

Federica fell silent and lowered her eyes again.

'Nothing that happened in the *pensione* lasted very long. The faces kept changing all the time as well.'

She stopped and looked at her father with a defiant air.

'When I was ill and we came here, I thought I was expecting a baby.'

Forte started but tried to cover it up.

'But I wasn't.'

'Did you want a baby?'

'Not at first. Never. I was afraid of having to tell all of you about it.'

'Why did you never tell us?'

They looked at each other without speaking.

'Why?' he asked impatiently. 'Why didn't you talk? Why didn't you talk between yourselves? What's the point of living like that, keeping everything separate?'

'It's always been like that for me.'

'What do you mean?'

'We always talk of little things, all separate from one another. We're embarrassed to put things together: different moments, the people we meet. Everything's so different from everything else. I often wanted to ask Marco what he did all day when we weren't together, but I was embarrassed. I was too embarrassed to ask my professor to explain things, to ask people in the street the way; there were some days I was embarrassed just to look them in the eyes. But if you stop trying to put all the moments in your life together, then you no longer get embarrassed about anything. I've never been embarrassed about anything ever since I stopped trying.'

She stared at him defiantly again.

'You couldn't have done it. You always go to the same places, you always see the same people, all just like you. So it's easy, there's no problem. But this is something I know more about than you. You don't see people, you don't meet them.'

She gave a trembling smile. 'Whereas I felt fine with anyone. It only took me a few days to understand how they worked. The very first day at the *pensione* was tough. There are a lot of people sleeping in the same rooms, some of them quarrel at times, there are others who aren't well. We didn't make love. You can't immediately understand the way people talk there. You don't know how to treat them. But it didn't take me long to understand. For example you must never ask anybody how they earn their living, where they get their money from. In our circles it's normal to ask people about their work. But there it's something you just mustn't do. And you mustn't let yourself think that the rooms are ugly either. After a while you get to like them. It was like that at the university for me as well. Always. During exams or when the professor was talking. You always have to say something original to them. In order to be original I used to study the footnotes. Now I can't remember a single exam, a single book. You always have to pick up other people's ways of doing things. Then there are times when you simply need to avoid reacting to things you see. If you have the right attitude towards things, if you really feel that things are all free to get along in their own way, then everything can be all right. In my room . . .'

She paused for a moment to force back her tears.

'There I felt better. I used to think of that journey, you remember, I told you about it. I'd talked to Marco about it too. He'd bought a map of the whole world. It was hanging up in the room in front of the bed. Every day he changed his mind and thought he'd go to a different place. He was very superficial. So was I when I was with him. With you one always has to be so intelligent. But I've discovered that both of you pretend. He used to say that all he wanted to do with me was make love. He was lying. Like you. You never wanted anyone close to you, but up on the mountain it was different. And then as soon as you felt better, you started lying again. We always have to fight you, don't we? That's what you want. So if I'm hard towards you, you think I'm more intelligent than the others and come looking for me, right?'

'Federica, we can't talk like this,' he said desperately, taking a cigarette from the bedside table.

'Don't smoke,' she ordered firmly. 'You mustn't smoke, it's bad for you.'

Forte put the cigarette down. They stared at each other.

'Yes, there's no need to talk about these things,' she said slowly. 'I just want to know what's happened to Marco. You must help me. Stop asking me why I never said anything about him or why we went out together.'

She sighed and then for a moment sat there without breathing. She was staring out into the darkness of the garden. Forte picked up the cigarette again without looking at her.

'Try not to smoke,' she said without turning.

Forte angrily threw the cigarette into the air. Federica turned and looked at him in surprise.

'I can't give up,' he justified himself. 'The idea that I can't really makes me angry. Now I've made my mind up. I hate being addicted.'

They stared at each other for a moment in silence.

'It takes a bit of time to stop thinking about it altogether,' she said.

'Rubbish. It's a question of mind over matter. If you want to, you give it up.'

'Marco used to smoke all the time. He was always on the look-out for a cigarette. They all smoked a lot there. That Somalian girl smoked three packs a day and was always coughing. So was Marco. He wasn't afraid of getting ill.'

'Because he never really had been.'

'No, I don't think it was that. He wasn't afraid of ruining his health by smoking or anything like that. But he was afraid of a lot of other things that don't bother us. Being on his own for example. When I left him, he would always get someone to accompany him wherever he wanted to go. He always wanted me to leave him in somebody else's company.'

Federica sat hunched up in the armchair, with her face resting on her knees, and looked at him.

'How can he have disappeared? What do you think?' she whispered.

'He could have gone off somewhere. Or he could have decided he didn't want to see you again. Maybe just because you always met up in this strange way and never told each other anything. He may have thought that he didn't even need to tell you. Or maybe he told the people at the *pensione* not to tell you where he was going.'

Federica was trembling slightly; she hugged her knees and chewed her lower lip.

'Towards the end he loved me, I think,' she said, almost inaudibly. 'So he can't have just gone off without telling me anything.'

'So towards the end things were different between you?'

'He asked me to go and live with him. He wanted to get a house. He asked me when he heard that Sandro was studying with me. But I couldn't live with him like that.'

'Why not?'

Federica started to tremble more noticeably. 'Outside that room I didn't know him. He bothered me. He was a stranger. There were so many normal things he didn't care about. I was afraid to lead the life he led. In fact I didn't even know what that life was. It was all so ugly there. It didn't bother him. I wanted to go back home, I didn't want to go anywhere with him. I couldn't.'

She repeated this sorrowfully, burying her face in her hands as she always did when emotion prevented her from speaking.

'He wasn't very much like you then, was he?' he asked, to get her speaking again.

'Yes, he was, very much. Once, at the beginning, he said that we'd met up that first time at the university because we were both looking for someone to make love with. In the room we were the same,' she said, gazing at a spot on the wall as if she were trying to remember. 'When we started thinking of this journey and he bought the map, everywhere seemed so close. You know how maps make the world look tiny. All the more so because he'd gone and bought a geological map instead of a political one by mistake. So it didn't even have the different colours for the countries, or the names of the cities, just the geological zones. I don't know why I'm telling you all these unimportant things. Maybe because they were very important to us and nothing else happened.'

'Where did you want to go together?' he asked.

'I wanted to go to India.' She looked up at him. 'I know it's not very original. A cliché perhaps. Anyway I wanted to go there because I'd just taken the Indian philosophy exam. It's the only exam I can remember anything about. While I was studying for it, I could imagine the country and the people. It was the first time. It seemed to me that there one would get to the essence of things. Or so I imagined, at any rate.'

'What do you mean, the essence of things?' he asked, unconsciously reaching out for the pack of cigarettes on the table.

Federica followed the movement of his arm. Their eyes met.

'Shall we smoke half each?' he suggested.

Federica nodded. Forte lit the cigarette. He took a few drags, then remembered the question he'd asked her.

Federica watched him smoke.

'What does the essence of things mean?' he asked her again.

'Maybe like the way things were between Marco and me,' she said, blushing. 'But maybe it's not true at all. Perhaps people just die of hunger there. That's what everyone says, and it's probably true then. When you want to go to a country like that, people tell you you're attracted by something negative, by their hunger because you've never experienced it. They're very convincing when they say this. So I never talked about it. After all, there are always more arguments to destroy what a person feels than there are to explain it. So they must have been right.'

'Who says this is so?'

'Everyone. At home as well. But you can read it everywhere. It's something you just know. You know it yourself too. You've often talked about it, about the infantile longing people have for mystical things. So it's better to say you're going somewhere else. A place whose attractions are easier to explain. But it's not so easy to find one.'

Forte breathed in the smoke with a pleasure that momentarily liberated him from the anguish of the situation. 'Yes,' he said, blowing it out again, 'what people write isn't that important. After all, people write about everything.'

He paused, the cigarette midway to his mouth. His mind was a whirl of quick, tumbling thoughts: about this journey and all the possible arguments in favour of it, against it, alternatives to it, about the longing for mystical things, what one said about them, why one talked about them; all the essential items of information flipped through his mind in rapid succession – with the exception of one vital piece: what he himself thought of his daughter's possible trip to India.

He stubbed his cigarette out angrily.

'You didn't let me have a single drag,' she said.

'Oh, sorry, I didn't feel like smoking it any more. I wasn't thinking.'

'It doesn't matter,' she said. 'You're very good if you really don't feel like smoking already. You're not physically addicted then.'

'That's not true at all,' he said. He tried to meet her eyes. He ought to add something to make her understand how wrong she was. He couldn't find the words.

Federica wasn't looking at him. Her eyes were wandering around her parents' room. She gazed at the mirror with the gilded frame which hung between the pale wooden wardrobe and her mother's secretaire.

In the three drawers her mother kept her silk blouses and the bright-coloured pullovers she was so fond of. Silvia and Caterina used to borrow her clothes and gaze at themselves in the mirror. Federica had never worn her mother's clothes.

Her eyes roamed over the bed where her father lay: it stood in the corner, with its pillows heaped one on top of the other: green, beige, brown. These colours are always to be found in houses with style. The rooms in the *pensione* had different colours.

Her eyes dropped down to her father, then to her hands on her knees. She started talking with an effort. 'Yes, you're right. It's a very long way away, there's no point in thinking of it. I can't remember anything else. When I came home after lectures and you weren't there, Mamma would be wandering round the house. I could hear her from my room. It was all fine, just fine. I'd come home, start studying. Mamma was there.'

She paused for a moment.

'I wasn't nostalgic about him. I never thought of him when I was at home. When we weren't together I forgot he existed. I always forget things as soon as I've done them, even exams. So in the end I know nothing. But when there's an exam on, it's as if I knew everything, it has the same effect.'

She looked up at her father. Forte saw her large eyes, glimmering with unshed tears.

'Now everything reminds me of him. I can't remember what happened. I must have done things I don't remember.'

She broke off and with one hand wiped away the tears rolling down her cheeks.

'How could I have failed to love him? To ask him things? How could I have behaved like this?'

For the first time since he'd read the diary, Forte thought of the boy she was crying over. Up to that moment he'd imagined him as a threat overhanging her, as a brutish character who'd blundered his way into a story of normal people, an offshoot of his daughter's illness. Now for the first time he saw him as similar to her in some way.

They had made love together over an unknown period of time. A youth without a past, who lived in a *pensione*, was always on the move, knew about churches and nothing else, and made money in some mysterious way. Like so many people. He wandered round the university where he met a friend and a girl with whom he made love.

What category of social outcasts did Marco belong to? To some such category without a doubt. There was no other way one could explain his life spent between a *pensione* and the station, or his love for a girl – Forte's own daughter – of whom he had never asked questions or told anything. But that was what she had wanted as well. Forte tried to think it through calmly, without upsetting himself too much. Marco was a stranger. She had chosen him for this very reason. And now she felt this intensely close tie to a stranger.

'It's irrational,' he thought. 'One of those things that often happens to women.' He must go back to Rome and make enquiries. For a moment he ran through a mental list of journalist friends who could help him out. He'd go to the police only later – if at all. Marco. All they had was a name. But he lived in and around the station; one just needed to talk to the right people. The thought of the search made him feel tired. He missed his wife.

Marta used to wander round the house by herself; Federica stayed all alone in her room, a prey to sickness; he had sat pondering over his papers at the office like a monk. He thought of the green curtains that cut him off from the outside world. Of the smell of his papers. Of his relations with his employees. Of all his hard work and his achievements.

He looked at his hands which were trembling and then at her. She was sitting silently in front of him, waiting.

'Mind you, at least she's better now and talking,' he thought, as he felt his heart and his hands gradually calm down.

'When did you meet? Don't you remember?' he asked her. 'In the diary you said it was spring.'

Federica nodded.

'It must have been in May then, because that's when your diary finishes.'

'It didn't really finish there,' she mumbled. 'There were some more pages which I tore out. I don't know why.'

'May last year. You took the philosophy of language exam in October. You said the date's in your registration book. So you were together for six months in all, if it's true that you didn't see one another after the exam.'

'Six months,' she murmured, as if it had struck her for the first time. 'It's a long time.'

'A long time? Just six months?' he repeated in surprise.

'I thought it was less.'

'I thought it was much more from the way you talked.'

Forte gazed at her in amazement; she was smiling.

'I never really thought about it,' she said after a moment. 'Six months. It was a long affair then, almost normal.'

'There was the summer too. You didn't see each other over the summer. Not in July, because you were here.'

'Yes,' she broke in. 'We saw each other every day.

He always came and picked me up by the faculty building and when I left he gave me this.'

She stretched her leg out and took off her sock. Forte gazed at the silver circle round her ankle. He saw his wife's face on the beach; he heard her questions and his own reassuring replies.

'He can't have gone off without telling me anything,' she said, smiling excitedly.

She stopped and blushed. She touched the silver circle again gently, then quickly hid it. She squeezed her knees between her arms without looking at him.

'Why did he behave differently with you towards the end?' he asked.

'There was something he was frightened of and couldn't stop thinking about. When we were together, his mind would start wandering by itself and he wouldn't speak except to make remarks like that thing about the necropolis. He wanted me to stay longer with him. But I couldn't. I couldn't bear to see him acting so strangely and weakly. He'd never been like that before. At first he never even liked me to drop in on him unless we had a date. I couldn't bear this change in him. I told him that I had to study, I had to go home. I can't believe it now. Now that I just want to have his baby, give up my studies and stay with him.' It all came out in one rush, and she sat trembling, squeezing her knees.

'Don't say such irration . . .' he responded. He broke off and wiped his brow with one hand. 'This kind of talk gets you nowhere.'

'Yes, you're right. You're always right. It gets me

nowhere,' she repeated sadly. 'It's all wrong. But at least – this is what I've realised here in Ischia – at least I know what I have to do with this weight I feel dragging me down inside. And now I wouldn't even be afraid of disappointing you. It wouldn't bother me at all.'

'That isn't possible, Federica. I love you too much.'

'Anyway I'm not expecting a baby. And I don't even know where the person I'd like to have it with is.'

Part 3

Twenty-Six

They were walking along side by side through an infinite expanse of barren fields. The naked earth and trees, a uniform and sullen ash-grey as far as the eye could see, began to take on colour. Blotches of scarlet, like paint dripping on to a canvas, blossomed at random in the landscape around them, subsequently fading into lighter shades of pink and red, until the whole scene was swathed in purple – a supernatural purple, one that had never been seen before. Forte thought: 'I'm ill, that's why everything looks purple. There's no such purple in nature. It doesn't exist. Landscapes shouldn't be painted in colours that don't exist. Trees have always been green, not purple.'

He tried to consider the matter calmly as they walked through this universal purple, but in fact he was frightened. The purple gave no signs of giving way: it seemed to have set in and to have found its natural shade in every clod of earth, every twist in the trunks. He looked up to see if the sky had changed colour too: it was a light purple. He looked

241

down at his shoes: they were purple like the rest of his body. He felt lost. He gave a sidelong glance at the purple legs of his fellow-traveller: they strode forward firmly, as if nothing had happened. So he mustn't slacken either, nor must he let it appear that he was worried about what was happening. It was perfectly normal for everything to have turned purple. It wasn't even ugly. Perhaps someone had spilt some chemical substance over the world.

'They've done it for our own good,' he thought. Perhaps because first they overdid things with the green, and now, trying to put things right, they've overdone it with the purple. It's not always easy to put things right. But they'll straighten everything out gradually, and then only the objects that are supposed to be purple will be left that way. They'll carry out their surveys, they'll send me the statistics regarding the excessive density of purple, the list of objects affected by purple, and all the papers that need signing and I'll deal with them straight-away. And so everything will get back to normal. There are too many hold-ups. The dead branches need lopping. I'll have to talk to Bosio and issue my instructions, give clear regulations on the use of colours.'

As he thought about what needed doing he ceased to observe the purple landscape around him and the legs moving in step with his. His fears were thus assuaged. He began to think that, all things considered, one couldn't state with absolute certainty that this purple everywhere was abnormal. Who was to say it was abnormal? Why should trees be green? Now they were purple. It was as simple as that.

He walked along, reassuring himself, but in fact deep down he felt that there was no real justification for the colour things had taken on and he realised that in some ways it was worrying. But there was no way of talking about it to the person by his side. He gave another quick glance at those legs: they were still striding along calmly. No, it wasn't possible to talk about it. What would he say to his companion? 'Don't you think there's something odd happening?' Or: 'Weren't the trees green once?' 'You don't have today's paper by any chance?' No, he couldn't do it. It would be impossible to prove to him, once they had got on to the subject, that the real colour of trees was green, and that something was definitely up.

He was sweating and his heart was beating irregularly. He gazed at the purple curve of the distant horizon, the violet expanse that faded into the lighter purple of the sky. He felt a growing fear of some appalling event about to take place and at the same time he longed to witness it.

The horizon began to move away from him, to slide backwards. As they walked on, the trees, the fields and the rivers around them began to shrink: at a glance they could take in the full extent of the rivers from their sources to their mouths; they could see whole cities and at the same time every tiniest lane and house within them. The horizon didn't slacken, it continued to slide backwards, leaving further space for the eye to roam over yet more landscapes, more lands, houses and rows of trees, which in turn at once shrank, revealing themselves as contained within a larger space which a second later was revealed as contained within something else. And all the time everything remained visible down to its minutest detail. Until finally, from the vantage point of the plain they were crossing, the whole planet was reduced to a manageable size for his eyes.

He trembled with fear. He reached out for the other person's hand and gripped it hard without looking at him because he couldn't tear his eyes from what he was seeing. The hand, inside his own, shrank until it became that of a small child.

He turned towards him: the child's face strained upwards as he gazed at the sky; he was wet and shivering with cold. His hand had a smooth, oily consistency which Forte recognised but couldn't remember from where. He held it firmly between his own two hands so that it wouldn't slip away, leaving him to face that terrifying event alone.

'Are you cold?' he asked.

'Yes, of course. Now I'm cold. Everyone's cold now,' the child said without looking away from the sky. 'But it was just as I thought, you see, everywhere was close to everywhere else and you could even have touched them with your hands. It's just that now we've got very little time to do so, while before we had loads. But they always have to make you die without telling you first. Look.'

With one hand he pointed up at the sky while the other gripped Forte's hand harder; he closed his eyes momentarily out of fear. Forte raised his face slowly towards the sky. Other planets could be seen just like theirs, all of them purple and rolling on ellipses of different dimensions. It was a frightening and beautiful spectacle.

Suddenly, the purple sphere of the planet nearest to theirs started to slow down; it came to a gradual halt, oscillating on its axis like a spinning top, just above their heads. Forte then realised that the smaller planets had stopped as well and were quivering above them like lampshades before an earthquake. The first one, right in front of them, split off from the others. It rolled towards them, increasing in size as it advanced. Forte thought that it wasn't fair that the child should have lived so briefly. He picked him up, and pressed the tiny head hard against his shoulder. The light breathing of the child on his neck banished all his fear. He looked for as long as possible and then closed his eyes.

He thrashed his arms about, tried to sit up but fell back on to the pillow. His heart was hammering inside his chest. He opened his eyes. He realised he had been crying in his sleep. His hand groped for the light on the bedside table. He could hear his wife's steady breathing. He recalled that other breathing in his dream. He managed to switch the light on and turned towards her: she lay with her mouth half-open. She had taken a sedative and was sleeping heavily and unnaturally. He pulled himself to a sitting position.

It happened every night. He didn't know how long he'd been dreaming that same dream now; he always woke up to find his wife asleep. As he looked at her his mind ran over the nightmare which he knew down to the slightest detail by now, and he thought of the child he lost at every reawakening. He had refused to take sedatives like her. He actually desired the dream, the nocturnal reawakening and the subsequent solitary reflections. He looked at his wife again. She had grown old. These last few years had marked her face more than all the others they had spent together. Her skin had thickened, and the bags under her eyes gave her a long-suffering expression even when asleep.

He looked away from her and stared at his hands: the tremor had remained with him, along with the insomnia, the nightmare and the weariness. He tried to remember when he had first noticed the tremor in his hands. It had been on Ischia, three years earlier. Perhaps when he'd woken up on Epomeo or even before that. He couldn't recall. There were many things from that time that he couldn't remember exactly. But he had his notebook. Occasionally, when he saw some violent scene in a film on television – he often watched television now that he no longer worked – or when his eyes fell on some drop-out huddled at a street corner while he was shopping, fragments of his daughter's story would come to mind.

As soon as he got back home, or at night in bed while his wife was asleep, he would open the locked drawer by the bed and take out the notebook which contained an account of the whole story. He never read it in front of his wife.

They had talked about it in the early days, just after Federica had left them. For several nights, alone in the house, they had discussed it and she had cried. Then he realised that his wife couldn't think about it without getting muddled. She couldn't believe in the truth. It hadn't penetrated her life, and those conversations merely confused her. Gradually, with the combined help of sedatives, of her love for her distant daughter, of the attention of the other two with whom she talked in turn about their sister, of the letters they received and the phone-calls, she had managed to create her own version. The daughters didn't know the truth and so couldn't contradict her. Sometimes she repeated it in front of him as well but his pitying gaze would reduce her to silence. She would at once change the subject and talk about little Marco, now a year old, or the beautiful house Federica had restored with her husband in the centre of the foreign town where she now lived.

Marta was especially proud of little Marco. She loved him more than her other grandchildren. She often said to Caterina and Silvia – forgetting that they were her daughters as well and mothers of her grandchildren – that Marco was clearly the most intelligent and precocious of them all. As intelligent as his mother had been when she was small.

Forte was glad to see his wife survive those events so well; he was happy to see her go out with her daughters and to know that she had regained a full intimacy with her youngest.

But he had his notebook. On certain afternoons

he would sit there alone in the living-room with an unread book in his hand. Silence hung over the house, broken only by the ticking of the grandfather clock in the hall. He would look all around the room, over all the familiar objects, the silver tree with their photos hanging on every branch; finally, with trepidation, his eyes would settle on the photo of Federica.

He remembered looking at it on another occasion, just before his decision to set off with her three years earlier: her mouth was half-open in a smile, her hand raised to her forehead as she brushed back a strand of hair. He would wait for a few seconds before meeting her eyes. Then they would stare at each other in the silence of the deserted house.

And thus he would reminisce over their trip together, recalling the silent evenings they spent together, with him in an armchair holding an unread book – just as he was now – and her asleep on the sofa. The room on Mount Epomeo in which he had come round. Her caressing hands giving him courage. The night they'd spent in the same bed without embarrassment. And how he had subsequently driven her from his side again, as the ceaseless motions of his mind distracted and confounded him and made him forget her.

Afterwards, everything else had followed inevitably: his reading of her diary, their return to Rome, and, then the final outcome – or, as other people (friends, colleagues, newspapers) might have termed it: 'the whole truth about the matter.'

They hadn't been given the chance to call it anything. He had succeeded in saving her from this at least. He gazed at her smile in the photo. It had been his gesture of love. It consoled him for her absence, her premature marriage, his life nowadays. He had saved her.

He stretched out his hand towards the table, picked up the glass of water and a little silver packet. He swallowed down a pink pill with the water. He couldn't remember the name of every pill, just the colour together with the time he was supposed to take it. He sipped the water slowly, blessing the silence which was disturbed only by his wife's breathing. He put the glass down and stared at the wall. He thought back to the child in the dream. Their encounter lasted no longer than an instant before everything finished, and yet he was keenly aware of him, of the feel of his breath on his neck, of the words he addressed to him before fear sealed his eyes.

He sat up again in bed, moving gently so as not to wake his wife. She remained awake in the evening when he went straight to sleep. He stayed awake in the small hours while she slept. And thus they watched each other sleep.

He stretched his hand out towards hers, which lay clenched on the sheet. He drew it back without touching her; he gripped his left hand with his right, and managed to still the tremor.

Sooner or later he would have to get rid of his notebook. He couldn't leave it lying around after his death. Federica must never know the full story.

His wife would forget all about it; his daughters

would spare her the pain of going through his papers and thus they would find it. He had to get rid of it. Immediately.

He tried to breathe regularly and to stop thinking for a few seconds in order to recover the necessary lucidity. He stretched his hand out to the table again, picked up the silver packet and swallowed another pill. His heart slowed down after a burst of rapid throbbing.

Now he had to decide how to dispose of it. Should he tear up every page into tiny pieces and throw it all into the rubbish-bin? Or burn it in the fireplace? That was the only way to prevent anything from being found. He felt a sudden sharp pang in his heart. He remembered something else being burnt in the story recounted in the notebook. So yes, burning was the best thing for it.

He moved slowly across the bed and eased himself out of it, stretching one foot down to the floor at a time. He turned towards his wife: she hadn't moved. He took a little key from the top of a picture-frame and opened the drawer by his bed. He ran the tip of his finger over the black cover of the notebook, then took it out without looking at it, staring down instead at his bare feet which he slid into his slippers. He opened the door noiselessly. His wife wouldn't notice he had gone; she no longer reached out to him now that she was taking the sedatives.

He went into the living-room and turned on just two lights: one by the sofa and the other one on the table next to his daughter's photo. Federica's face lit up. He left the notebook on the sofa. He picked up some sticks and arranged them in a little stack in the fireplace, leaving an empty space below for the paper. He took some sheets of newspaper from a pile by the fire and screwed them into balls. The wood lay waiting by the side. He struck a match and set fire to the paper. He waited for the sticks and the paper to burn properly. Then he placed two logs in the grate, one leaning against the other, without quenching the flame.

With the notebook in his hand he sat down on the sofa opposite his daughter's photo. His eyes flickered towards the fire: it was burning nicely; then they moved towards Federica's face which gazed at him, as if expecting something from him. At last he looked at the notebook in his hands. He opened it, wondering whether there was any plastic in the cover or not. He couldn't stand the smell of burning plastic. He looked at the last sentence and then at all the others on the last page. It was absurd to re-read it – he knew every single line. The idea of having to burn it provoked a strange feeling in him. He thought of the boy, Marco. He ran his finger over the lines of writing. For one moment he felt as if he were touching the boy's life just as one touches a face or a hand. Then he thought of the child in the dream. All things considered, it was right to read it before burning it. Perhaps he would at last be able to give the child in the dream Marco's face.

He looked up at his daughter in the frame. The light fell on her face and made it cheerful. He looked down at the first line in the notebook: he would re-read it for the last time and not think about it again. There would be no need to add another piece of wood.

Twenty-Seven

I have resigned. Bosio has temporarily taken my place. The board will meet in a week's time, pay their respects to me and replace me. The speech of thanks has been prepared by Migliani, the cultivated head of our design and projects office. He read it out to me to see how it sounded the day before I left: it was moving and well-written. A pity he's had to spend all his life in the design office of a company that doesn't need designs.

Before leaving I had a word with Bosio. I gave him some advice, some of the tricks of the trade. The experience I've accumulated is only of any help to myself; I have no idea how to teach anyone else my job. While I was waiting, I was wondering what to say to him and I couldn't think of anything beyond a few light remarks. But when he sat down in front of my desk, as he'd done on countless mornings, I simply couldn't joke. He looked tense, as if shaken by the fact that I was going, leaving him in charge.

I should have given him some reassurance but I don't have the technique, it's something I've never done. So I just suggested a few little tricks.

I've never given any more than the bare gist of my thoughts on the best of occasions – indeed, often the very opposite since I feared that my thoughts were too uncertain. Nowadays I feel that if everyone were to admit their doubts, there would be a good deal more certainty around. So, in the end, I told him nothing. I advised him to exchange the velvet curtains for some more transparent material.

I started writing this notebook to recount what happened to my daughter and to the boy who was with her. I wrote something else a long time ago. A little story of infidelity of no importance. It helped me to deal with problems arising from work and middle-age. I returned to this notebook when we started to get worried about Federica's silence. And I've come back to it again now, when it's all over and done with, without any apparent traces. But this time I want to write about those two. Everybody knows that retired people spend their time doing nothing. There's nothing interesting to write about. I couldn't have gone on working; I'm ill and I was unable to stop thinking about my daughter, who lives so far away, and about the boy.

There are many ways of imagining him. She must now remember him in a special way. Now that she lives with her husband in a foreign town.

She'll be reminded of him whenever she calls her baby, whenever she comforts him when he's crying. We all have some similar nostalgia for a feeling that doesn't fit in with our current way of life and has hence been discarded.

I have committed no crimes in my life. There is only one that weighs on me, something that befell my daughter and about which she knows nothing. Between the person who knows about the deed and the person who commits it, there is an ever-widening gap. Every deed hurtles into the void, severing itself from all possibility of comprehension.

Federica gave up studying philosophy. She took a course in simultaneous translation and got married. The doctors told us that for a few years she mustn't think too much. Philosophy is bad for anyone who has suffered a trauma.

Nobody knows where the boy is. He's probably together with that other one who lay stretched out on the ground.

'Thou dost preserve the stars from wrong; and the most ancient heavens, through Thee, are fresh and strong.' It's by the English poet William Wordsworth. Federica kept repeating it and couldn't remember the name of the author. I found it in her book of Indian philosophy. Now that she's so far away, I feel that her longings, her unjustified love for me, and our trip together are all lost for ever. Now she's a prematurely married young lady and a mother.

I recall fragments from her diary, one sentence especially: 'I don't know why I tore the pages out, I don't know what happened that day.'

We haven't told her anything. What point was there in telling her the truth? As a punishment? For what crime? She knew nothing. Federica always expunged what she did immediately. In her mind nothing happened until Marco disappeared. Maybe for this very reason we should have told her the truth, made her suffer and thus get over it. But suppose she hadn't been able to bear the truth? She'd recounted what happened the day after the philosophy of language exam in her diary, in the missing pages. This is what Marta and I thought. We stayed awake whole nights discussing it. We had found out the truth and wondered what to tell her. Why had she torn the pages out? Because she was afraid someone might find them? Because she was afraid to re-read them? Maybe she started to believe that such a terrible thing had never happened, not to her, nor to Marco, nor to Sandro. So she tore the pages out, started to forget and to fall ill at the same time. We lied to her in order to get her to leave.

A few weeks after we got back from Ischia I found out what had happened that day. No boy by the name of Marco who lived in the way she'd described had disappeared: not according to the police, the owners of the *pensione* Aurora, Pino the 'boss' of the household-appliances store, and the few Somalians I managed to talk to. They all held their tongues, through indifference, complicity or fear. Later I met some of these people again and in the end they told me what they knew, except for Pino, the 'boss'. Pino has never done anything but sell household appliances, all under regular licence – so he claims. He had never met Marco or Sandro.

I thought of Sandro's vacant stare as he sat in his white chair in room 114 at the clinic of Villa Claudia; of Federica, now far away; and of the other two, who were beyond all help.

Federica had never told anyone her surname. Marco and Sandro had read it just once in her registration book. Nobody at the *pensione* knew anything about the girl who used to follow Marco up the stairs. Nobody knew Sandro's surname either. Marco had introduced him as a friend who had come from France. And so both Federica and Sandro had managed to escape that day and cover their tracks. Marco, however, was already lost.

Federica went back to the *pensione* several times to look for him, but she didn't know the places he trafficked. All she could do was talk to the owners of the *pensione*, who wanted nothing to do with it. Then she stopped going there, tore the pages out and fell ill. I think this is the order of events.

After I'd spoken to Sandro's parents and met

him in that room in the clinic, I decided not to look into it any further.

Federica was safe. We sent her off with a dramatic lie but nothing compared with the truth: the boy she'd met on the wall by the faculty building and then borrowed a cigarette from, the boy whom she had visited every day for six months in a hotel room, and about whom, despite everything, she knew nothing, had died in a motor-bike accident. I told her that I'd heard everything from Sandro's parents, that Sandro had been with him when the accident happened. I think she would have believed anything.

Now that she's left us, my two elder daughters often come to see Marta. They give me a quick kiss on arrival and departure. I think of how she embraced me so naturally in the shelter at the top of the mountain and slept beside me when I was ill. I've never done anything like this for any of the three of them. Not even for her, though I loved her more than the others, I don't exactly know why. Maybe, in my present solitude, I've come to understand something. I've never managed to love them as I would have liked to. I knew it would have been the right thing to do. If I actually thought about it, I knew it, but I never *felt* it. I've always imagined a life without any limitations, without children, without death. I've not been a father. I tried to be open and kind to them, I think. I was worried that they wouldn't manage to carve out their own lives, so I always supposed that none of them would notice my shortcomings. It is no consolation for me to have understood this now that they've gone. Marta, who has remained, has drifted away from me too in the silence of our home.

Let's get back to a strict account of the facts, it's easier. After Federica had left, I spent whole days wondering why on earth nobody had reported Marco's disappearance. I found it hard to believe, just as she had done, that he had ever existed.

Sandro had already been admitted to the clinic when I went to see his parents in the stationery shop. He had told them about a girl who had been there when the thing happened, so they weren't surprised to meet me. We went to their house to talk things over, not far from the shop. He said very little; she told me what they had heard from Sandro, about what had happened the day after the philosophy of language exam. We all tried to work out just why Marco should have decided to take Federica and Sandro with him into the deserted subway and make them witnesses of the appalling scene. Who was the man who set fire to the African sleeping there while they watched? And why did he shoot Marco immediately afterwards? It was an un-fathomable affair like a thousand such cases one reads about in the newspaper or hears discussed in court. Perhaps Marco was supposed to act as look-out while the other man wiped out an African who hadn't stuck to his side of the bargain, a man who had nothing to lose and might have reported their traffickings. But why had Marco agreed to take part in a murder? And why had he decided to take them with him on that particular occasion? Perhaps he was already too deeply involved and couldn't get out of it. Or perhaps it was the first time they had involved him in a murder.

Sandro managed to escape with Federica. Marco yelled to them to run the instant he was shot. Sandro ran and just before he left the subway he turned and saw Marco's body lying on the ground. Then he fled, forgetting all about Federica. So they split up almost immediately, and managed to get safely away. Sandro told his parents that Marco never involved them in his affairs but on that occasion he'd said angrily: 'You both took an exam yesterday, so today I'll show you mine.' So it had been an exam. To become what? At any rate he had failed. He'd made a mistake in bringing two strangers. Maybe, at the last moment, he felt he might be able to pass the exam on his own. Maybe he was tired of living that life without talking about it; maybe he hated them because they'd stayed out of it. Sandro had wandered around town before going back to his parents; he was too scared to return to the *pensione*.

This was what they were able to tell me. In

tears, they begged me to keep quiet about it. My son and your daughter are innocent, they said. They didn't know. My son is ill, he's on drugs, he never talks about it now.

And in fact he didn't talk about it. Only when I murmured the name of Federica did he look at me for an instant before lowering his eyes to the clean handkerchief he was fiddling with.

There was no record of any murder committed on the day after the date in the registration book; no body had been found in a deserted subway. After wiping out the African, that man shot Marco. Perhaps it had been decided beforehand. Or perhaps he shot him when he saw Sandro and Federica hiding in the distance. Perhaps Marco told them to watch from a distance and the man spotted them and chased them without managing to catch them. Afterwards, with someone else's help, he got rid of the two bodies.

The story Sandro's parents told me tied in with that mysterious hallucination of Federica's, which she ended up by dismissing: 'a nightmare with people running from a fire.' Maybe she and Sandro had run away immediately, as soon as they saw the fire. Fled in horror.

The owners of the *pensione* Aurora didn't lie a second time. Probably they suspected it was dangerous to go on saying nothing. I told them I was Marco's father. They pretended to believe me. I wasn't the kind of person they were used to dealing with and they were scared. They didn't know anything about Marco's disappearance but they had kept his stuff.

It was all stored in a tartan travelling-bag with a broken shoulder-strap. The bag and the clothes it contained showed good taste. Shirts, cotton trousers, good-quality pullovers. I recognised something of Federica's old-fashioned taste. There were some very battered suede shoes; underwear, a scarf, a map of Rome, two of Federica's and Sandro's philosophy books. A small bag with soap, razor, shaving-cream and eau-de-Cologne. The whole thing could have belonged to any student on holiday. There were no documents, just two photos inside a plastic document-holder together with three cinema tickets. They were both on one strip of paper, passport-size, very dark, obviously taken in the street in some automatic machine: in the first one, Federica was looking into the camera with a slight smile and her cheek was being kissed by a boy seen sideways on; in the other one, the same boy's face, with a serious expression, was lined up next to Federica's. The boy was Marco. I couldn't describe him now. In her diary Federica wrote that he was short but carried himself as if he were all muscles. It was true. I can add – she couldn't see it because she was too young – that he had a shy expression. A boy with an expression of that kind couldn't hurt anyone.

I threw the bag away. It was the only proof that Marco and Federica knew one another, possibly the only proof of his existence. The bodies have never come to light.

The notebook ended here. A letter had been slipped into the last page. Forte took it out and started to read it, as he did every time he opened the notebook.

Dear Papà,

Sorry I haven't written for so long. Marco keeps me very busy and the days go by without a free moment. He's been walking by himself for a few days now. He isn't afraid so long as I hold my hands out towards him. If he feels that I'm too far away, he looks around with a lost expression and sits straight down on the ground. One year old is such a wonderful age. Every day he does something different. It seems incredible that he learns so quickly. He's very cheerful and sweet-tempered. We spend the day together in the public gardens here and sometimes, when it's not too cold, we take some food along and stay out the whole day. Before I had Marco I didn't think I would ever be able to love someone and be so involved with him. As I write, he's sitting opposite me, playing with his dummy, and every so often he waves as if he wanted to add something to the letter himself. He's just sneezed. I'm going to clean his nose. On the phone Mamma said you were more relaxed now. You mustn't worry about me. I'm happy enough here. I'm not going to look for a job until Marco goes to nursery-school. I feel that this time devoted entirely to him is a miracle both for my life and his. We wander round the town together, we pop into the cake-shops (we have two or three breakfasts). In the gardens, Marco plays with the earth, dabbles his hands in the ponds, competes with the other children and every so often comes back to me to show me something, to be comforted or to make me laugh. I've rediscovered things with him: the smell of wet earth, the fresh water of the fountains we drink from. Yesterday the book I was reading ended up in the water, so now its pages are all yellow and crinkled. I read a lot again, even though I have to fit it into my odd free moments.

Dear Papà, you'll make fun of me and think I've become like every other mother; well, it's the truth and I'm not ashamed of it. I'm trying to keep hold of this time in my life and make it last as long as I can. I think I feel these things so clearly because of all that I went through in Rome. Now it seems a very long time ago. Everything's happened so quickly.

I often think of Marco. I keep remembering those unexpected words he came out with when we were at the *pensione*, that he wanted to marry me and have a baby. Sometimes I think my baby is the one he wanted. Sometimes that it's him as a baby.

But I think that it's only one's unexpressed

feelings that blur into one another like this, that slip from one person to another without ever finding peace. Feelings that have been lived, on the other hand, are as unique and unrepeatable as people are.

I would have made a terrible philosopher. I can never think in general terms: it's individual cases that attract me most. Nowadays I wouldn't even be capable of attempting abstract thoughts. I'd be afraid, perhaps because of my illness. If ever I find myself thinking about it, I suddenly feel as though I'm standing at the top of a high mountain and looking down into the void with a terrible sensation of vertigo. So I immediately try and get my mind back to the little things in my life. It's a limitation I have. After all, one oughtn't to be afraid of looking out from a mountain peak. It must be a wonderful sight. But I would need to be able to measure the distance from where I stand at the top of the mountain to the horizon in one glance. Otherwise, for a person like me, I think the best thing would be to go with someone else. That's how it is with Marco when we go out together; he shows the world to me and I show it to him. It seems pretty good to both of us. I miss you and love you,
Federica.

Twenty-Eight

He folded the letter up and slipped it between the last written page and the first blank page in the notebook. The flames were attacking the last piece of wood in the fireplace. It was still burning well. He thought of the man lying in the subway. Of the boy called Marco. Of the baby called Marco. Of the boy called Sandro in the clinic. Of Federica and her baby. Stories barely touched upon, with no apparent bonds between them. And he was left there in the sitting-room, all on his own, thinking them over. But then one only ever thinks things over when they *are* over. With the necessary detachment. He brought this line of argument to an abrupt halt. He didn't believe in such reasoning any longer. It came from nowhere, had no connection with anything that was happening around him; it was indifferent to the pain that marked every object in the room, that brooded over the clock-ticking silence.

'What use is this detachment to me now?' he thought angrily.

He swallowed saliva to quench his emotion as he

always did. Emotion can be dangerous to a person with a heart condition. He looked at his daughter's photo in the circle of the lamplight. He saw her walking through the public gardens of the foreign town with her baby. Now she had a bond. He felt a longing to be with her, to hold the child's free hand and walk along with him, just as he did with the child in his dream, strolling round the planet which had shrunk to a manageable size for their eyes.

He closed his eyes. He tried to imagine postponing – even for just one second – the terrible event that was to eliminate them together.

They walked hand in hand from one region to another. As they stepped over a river they got their feet wet, distracted by the sight of a frog and the vegetation at the bottom; if they raised their eyes they could see the mountain torrent, the source of the river now swirling round their toes and over the frog's webbed feet. It was easy to explain every-thing to the child; easy for him to understand. They walked along in this fashion, trying to slacken their pace; they wanted to draw out this last walk for as long as possible. But the planet ended abruptly and as soon as the child saw the point they had set out from, he almost came to a halt, afraid to reach it. Then Forte fancied that the little planet was beginning to grow again, so that the space between them and the end stretched out to infinity.

They walked on and the horizons rolled away from them; great tracts of space broadened around them, leaving little crumbs of earth, and the rivers swelled, leaving droplets of water. The child smiled. They were safe. They had a long long way to go yet. They didn't know exactly how far. They couldn't see their departure point any more. But it seemed endless because they could remember perfectly well how short it really was.

He held the notebook tightly in his hands. He wanted to ignore the hammering of his heart, the pain in his shoulder. The pills were far away, and so was his wife, asleep.

With his eyes closed, he felt he was lifting the child – just as he did in his dream; their breaths mingled. The irregular throbbing of his heart next to the strong impatient beat of the child's. He felt good.